THAT'S WHAT LOVE IS

BREWING LOVE & LATTES SERIES

AMY ROSE

Edited by Sierra Campbell - Editing by Sierra, Jenny Sims, Sarah Lamb
Cover Design by Fieriz Book Cover Design
Formatting Services by Disturbed Valkyrie Designs

ISBN: 979-8-9893447-2-7

AUTHOR'S NOTE

Content Includes:
Verbal / Emotional abuse by a parent.
Cancer / Death of a parent.

THAT'S WHAT love IS

I dedicate this to my younger self, the child who went through it all. I want to tell her that in this world of darkness, there is a beacon of light waiting to be discovered. It might take some time, but she will find it.

PLAYLIST

Your Daughter - Chase McDaniel
That's What Love Is - Alexandra Kay
For the Love of a Daughter - Demi Lovato
Daughter to Father - Lindsay Lohan
Piece by Piece - Kelly Clarkson
My Mind & Me - Selena Gomez

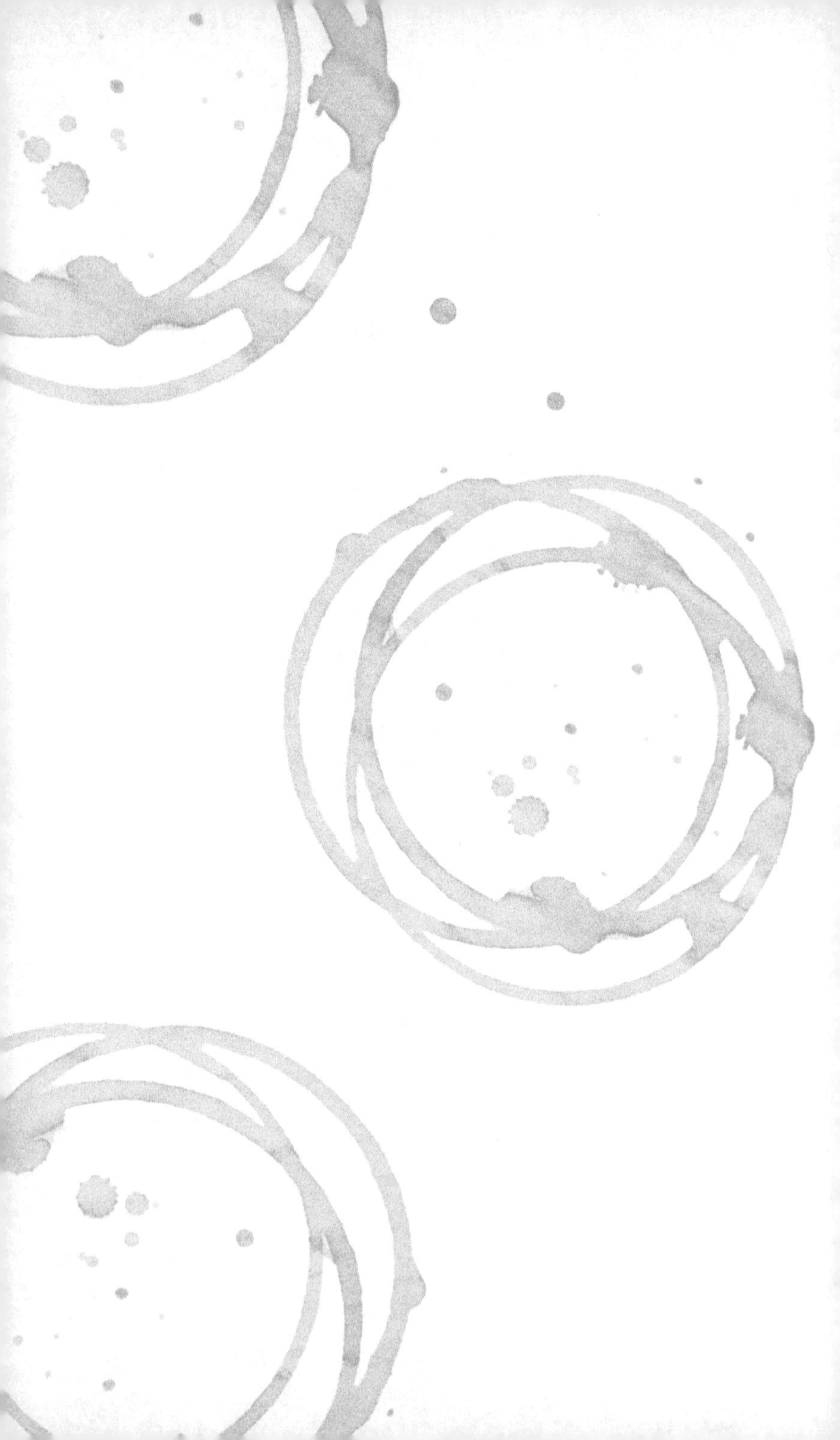

CHAPTER ONE

THE COFFEE SHOP BUSTLES WITH THE MORNING RUSH. I glance at my phone, frowning when I don't see any messages from my dad.

Sometimes, I go months without hearing from my dad, only for him to resurface and shower me with sweet text messages. It creates a glimmer of hope that he'll stop being so mean and cruel with his words. But that feeling fades as he reverts to his old ways, which happens within a month or two of being nice to me. When that happens, I typically cry myself to sleep, berate myself for falling into the same trap once more, and immerse myself in my work to avoid dwelling on it.

DAD

You're a bitch.

Cunt.

Go to hell.

Unlike with my phone, I'll never be able to erase those messages from my head.

I wipe down the espresso machine, my mind wandering to the excruciating hurt that I have yet to get used to. At just twenty-four years old, I've had years of emotional torment caused by my father's presence. The verbal abuse haunts me, lowering my sense of self-worth and leaving me wary of opening my heart to men. I stop speaking to him when he mistreats me. I can ignore him for months. But he always comes back.

DAD

I miss you.

Your daddy loves you.

I wish you would come down to the house some more. Maybe we can have a cookout.

Maybe I'm stupid, but hope continues to brew inside me that he may be changing. I always reply, saying I love and miss him back, and then and things are fine between us for a little while. He will message me a few times a week to check on me and see how I'm doing, But I'm still hesitant that he's actually changed, and I guard my heart and keep my messages short until he proves that he is worth it. Then I let my guard down.

Eventually, he gets drunk again. He has no reason to be so awful to me—no matter how he's feeling—but he still is.

I scrub the machine's surface a little harder, trying to wash away the painful memories. Each insult, each cutting remark from my father, has left indelible scars. While the scars from my past may not be immediately apparent, they've etched within me a sense of caution that colors my perception of love. I long for the kind of love that feels like a warm embrace, but I always seem to approach it with careful steps. I hesitate to fully open up to new possibilities, afraid of the unexpected plot twists that love can bring.

A woman walks up to the counter and asks, "Ma'am, can I get a refill?"

"Sure thing."

She thanks me as I pour coffee into her mug.

As I move to put the pot back onto the coffee maker, I see Scarlett—my best friend, boss, and the owner of the café—gesturing for me to come over.

She's been my best friend since the first grade. She has witnessed the verbal abuse from my dad and the meltdowns I've had from his horrible words. But she grew up with an awesome dad and will never understand. But that's okay. I wouldn't wish this feeling on my worst enemy. I can rely on her, and she does her best to support me. I love her for it.

"Hailey, you've gotta stop getting in your head at work," she whispers as I walk over to her.

"I'm sorry. My dad hasn't contacted me at all."

"Really? It's been four months."

"Yeah. Normally, it's about two, but it's longer this time, and I'm worried he may still be mad at me from the last argument we had."

"Not that it matters, but what did you say to him?"

"I basically said he needs to grow the fuck up and leave me the hell alone until he does." Scarlett widens her eyes, leans against the counter, and crosses her arms. "Hails, you don't need him. Plus, you have Ray—he's the only dad you need."

I sigh and look up at the ceiling. My eyes burn with the welling tears, my lip quivering with the effort of trying to swallow them down. "He's still my dad, though. Maybe I should just contact him and apologize."

"No, you don't owe him an apology. If he wasn't abusive in the first place, you wouldn't feel the need to apologize," she responds.

"That's true... but I still feel a pang of guilt for saying it."

"He hasn't messaged you for this long because he probably wants you to feel guilty. Don't let him control you."

"I'll try not to."

She gives me a hug. "I'm going to wipe down the tables."

As the last customer of the morning rush leaves, I take a moment to collect myself and push aside the haunting memories, doubts, and scars that have defined my existence for far too long.

The door chimes, and my gaze lands on a man entering the cafe. A dark blue plaid flannel hangs loosely over his white T-shirt, while his blue jeans and sturdy work boots complete the outfit. A baseball cap casually rests atop his brown hair, and his captivating blue eyes send a flutter of butterflies deep within me.

I put on my best customer service smile as he approaches the counter. "Welcome in! How can I help you today?"

"Hey, any recommendations for a coffee that will make my taste buds dance?" His playful remark brings a soft laugh to my lips.

"Well, if you're up for a little adventure, I'd suggest trying our signature caramel macchiato. It's a perfect blend of smooth espresso, creamy milk, and just the right amount of caramel sweetness."

"Sounds good. I'll take a small one to go, please."

"Four dollars, please."

He pulls a brown wallet from his back pocket and hands me a five-dollar bill. I click the screen on the cash register for it to open and place the money inside before closing it, his dollar in my hand.

"You can keep the change," he says.

"Thank you," I say, placing the dollar in my tip jar. I feel his gaze on me as I reach for the portafilter, causing my fingers to tremble and my heart to quicken. I fill it with freshly ground espresso and tamp it down, trying to keep my hands from showing how nervous he is making me. I place the portafilter in the espresso machine and pull the lever, filling the cup with a rich, fragrant shot of espresso.

The scent of freshly brewed coffee engulfs me, and I feel happy because I'm about to create something wonderful. I slide the cup beneath the frothing wand, the milk's silky surface shimmering as it heats.

His eyes hold mine for a lingering moment. "What would you say is the best thing to do around here? I haven't been in town for a while, and I'm looking for some recommendations."

My mind is racing to conjure up the highlights of the little town of Beaufort. "Well, it depends on what you're into. If you enjoy nature, we have some beautiful hiking trails just a short drive away. And if you prefer a more urban experience, the downtown area is filled with charming local shops, restaurants, and cultural events."

I reach for a to-go cup and pour the frothed milk from the pitcher. I watch as it fills the cup to the brim, creating light swirls in the rich espresso. I grab a lid to place over the cup and hand it to him.

"Here you go."

He takes the cup. "Thank you. I'm Eric, by the way."

"You're welcome, Eric. I'm Hailey, nice to meet you."

Eric nods with a smile, his eyes sparkling with genuine

interest. He takes the lid off, smells the coffee, and takes a sip before speaking. "This smells and tastes really great."

"Thank you. When was the last time you were here?" I ask.

"I left when I was ten."

"Oh, you moved with your family?"

He nods, placing his cup down on the counter in front of him. "Yeah, my mom got a new job after my dad passed away from a boating accident."

"Oh my gosh, I'm so sorry." I feel a little embarrassed talking with him about family when my own is so screwed up. I am careful to make no mention of mine.

"It's alright, life goes on, eventually," he responds.

I nod in agreement.

"See you around." He smiles and picks up his cup, then heads out the door. As soon as the door shuts, a small smile tugs at the corners of my mouth.

"Oh, hot damn, chica!" Scarlett screeches with a mischievous look in her eyes.

I jump at the sound of her voice and laugh. "Chill, girl. It was nothing."

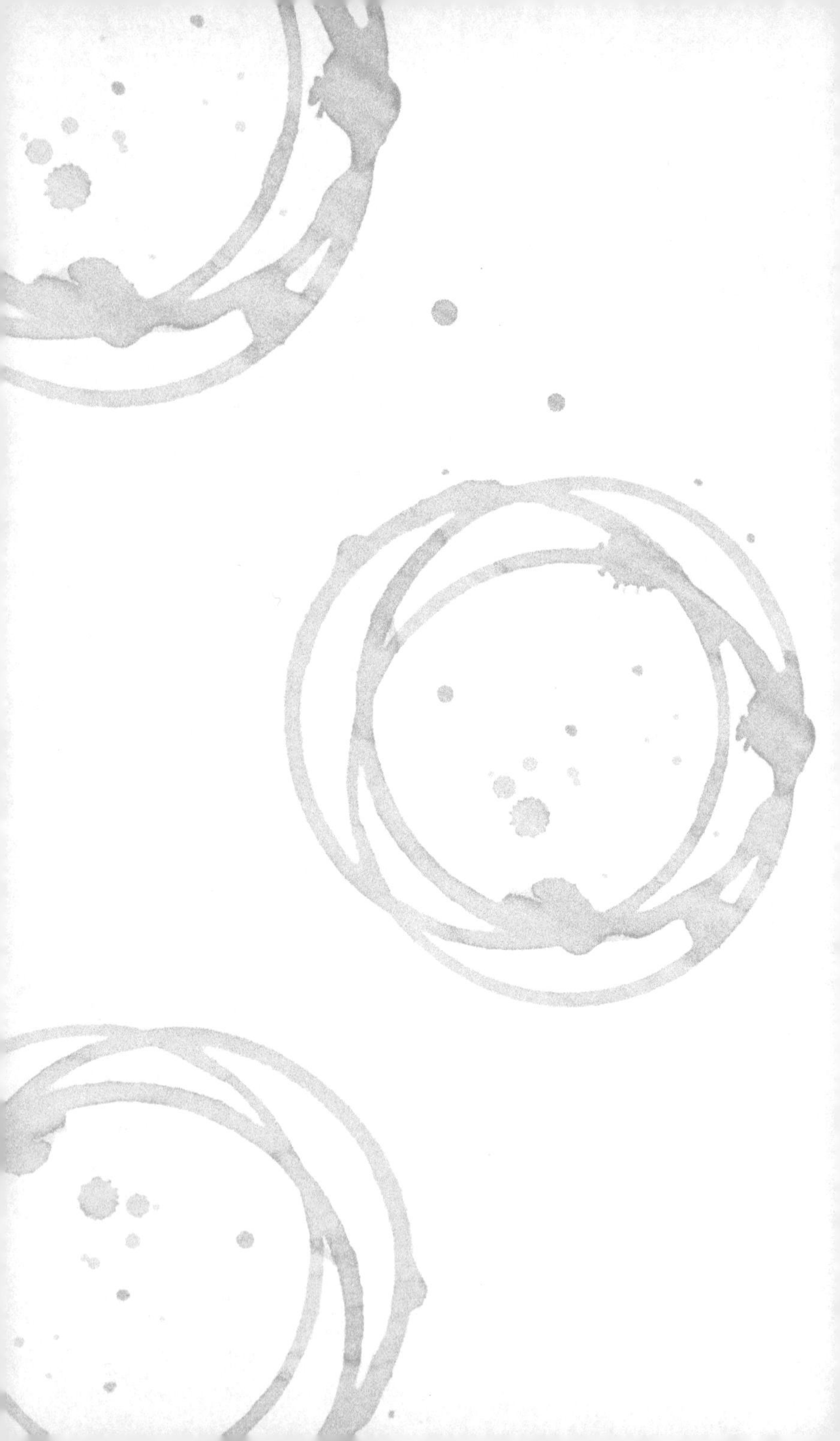

CHAPTER TWO

THE NEXT DAY, I SIT ON MY BED, SCROLLING THROUGH social media, when my phone dings. A notification flashes with the name "Dad" across the screen, and my heart drops to the pit of my stomach.

DAD

It's been a bit since we spoke, just checking in!

I stare at the message. Should I respond right now? I begin to type out a message but decide against it. *I don't need to send a message while my head is cloudy.* I lock my phone, toss it on the bed, and take a deep breath. I push the soft pink comforter off my legs, stand up, and walk toward the window, opening the blinds and looking outside. There it is —the only thing that can relax me right now—the view of the small pond across from my house, ducks already swimming around and dipping their heads into the water.

I walk toward my closet, its broken door triggering a memory of a breakdown I had in front of Scarlett. Any time my dad became cruel with his words, I'd shed some tears, and sometimes I would break down.

MY DAD HAS BEEN TREATING ME LIKE SHIT AGAIN. I FEEL THE energy welling up inside and need to find an outlet. "I can't handle this anymore, Scar. I can't!" I cry and lunge for the first solid thing I see: my closet doors. I channel my rage and frustration into the doors until one is off the hinges and the other has a few dents in it.

"Hailey, please calm down!" Her voice is faint and sounds far away, but I can still hear the panic.

"Hailey!" Scarlett yells.

I slowly came to a stop, my eyes burning with tears, and I collapsed to the ground. "Why me?" I cry out as I shove my head into my knees.

Scarlett's arm wraps around my shoulders as she pulls me into her chest.

I THINK ABOUT THAT MEMORY ALMOST EVERY TIME I LOOK at my broken closet doors. I haven't had the energy to replace or remove them.

My phone pings again, and I roll my eyes, knowing it's probably my dad. *Here we go.* I grab my phone and read another text from my dad.

DAD

I guess you don't want to speak to me. It's okay! I'll be changing my number tonight. You don't have to worry about me again!

With a deep breath, I hover my shaky thumbs over the keypad and type out a response.

ME

Sorry, been busy.

With a surge of frustration and resentment, I fling my phone onto the soft sanctuary of my bed. Wiping away the tears, I slip into my outfit. I put on my shoes, and the weight of the leather tethers me to the present.

I take a deep breath and grab my phone from the bed and my keys off the dresser. Their merry jingle brings a playful rhythm to the air. With my head held high, I walk out the front door, locking it behind me and sealing away any lingering doubts.

THE CHARMING CAFE GREETS ME AS I PULL INTO THE parking lot. This place, with its welcoming scent of freshly brewed coffee and the cheerful hum of patrons, has consistently been my sanctuary, a space brimming with companionship and comfort.

I swing open the door.

Scarlett immediately envelops me in a warm embrace. "How's it going, love?" she asks.

I return the hug, feeling the weight of the world lift from my shoulders in her presence.

"I'm okay," I mumble with a forced smile plastered on my face.

Scarlett looks at me with a discerning gaze, seeing right through my facade. Her concern is clear, and she knows me too well; she understands my highs and lows better than anyone else. Leaning in slightly, she continues in a softer tone, "You know you don't need to hide things from me… Did something happen? Has your father reached out to you?"

"Scarlett, I don't want to talk about it right now. Can we please just focus on work?" She nods.

I know she means well, but right now, I just need some space. No matter what challenges lie ahead, I know that I am surrounded by my best friend's love and understanding; with her, I can find the strength to weather any storm.

The familiar chime of the door draws my attention. I glance up, and my eyes lock with Eric, the guy from the day before. I can't help it—my cheeks are warm, and I know I must be blushing. My fingers tremble slightly, and I try to hide them under the counter.

Eric approaches the counter with a warm smile, his eyes twinkling with a hint of mischief. "Hey there, Hailey! Could I get a black coffee and a blueberry muffin?"

I chuckle. "Oh, look at you, remembering my name!"

He grins back. "Wouldn't want to mix up a name that belongs to a pretty face."

I blush, not expecting him to say that. "That'll be $4.50, please."

Eric hands me a ten-dollar bill, and our fingers momentarily brush against each other, bringing a little more warmth to my face. I place the money in the register and give him his change. As I swiftly prepare his order with practiced ease, I can't help but steal glances at Eric, feeling a strange mix of nervousness and anticipation. I place the steaming cup of coffee and the muffin before him.

As Eric takes a sip, he leans on the counter, his gaze sincere. "So, how are you today? Everything going well?"

A rush of excitement surges within me, and I can't help but respond with a wide grin. "Absolutely! It's a beautiful day."

His next words take me by surprise, stumbling forth from his lips as if caught in a rush. "You know, I really enjoyed talking with you yesterday, and… I was thinking, would you maybe want to, you know, go out for dinner sometime?"

Pausing for a moment, I notice his confidence waver slightly.

I offer a soft response, "Eric, I truly appreciate your kind words, but I'm not looking to date right now."

A flicker of embarrassment flashes across his face, and he quickly amends, " Uh, okay, how about we hang out sometime? As friends?"

To put him at ease, I offer a reassuring smile. "That would be nice."

A grin spreads across his face, and he gives me a quick wink before heading off to his next destination.

As my cheeks flush, I nervously nibble on my lip, internally admonishing myself. *Hailey, you don't need more on your plate right now.*

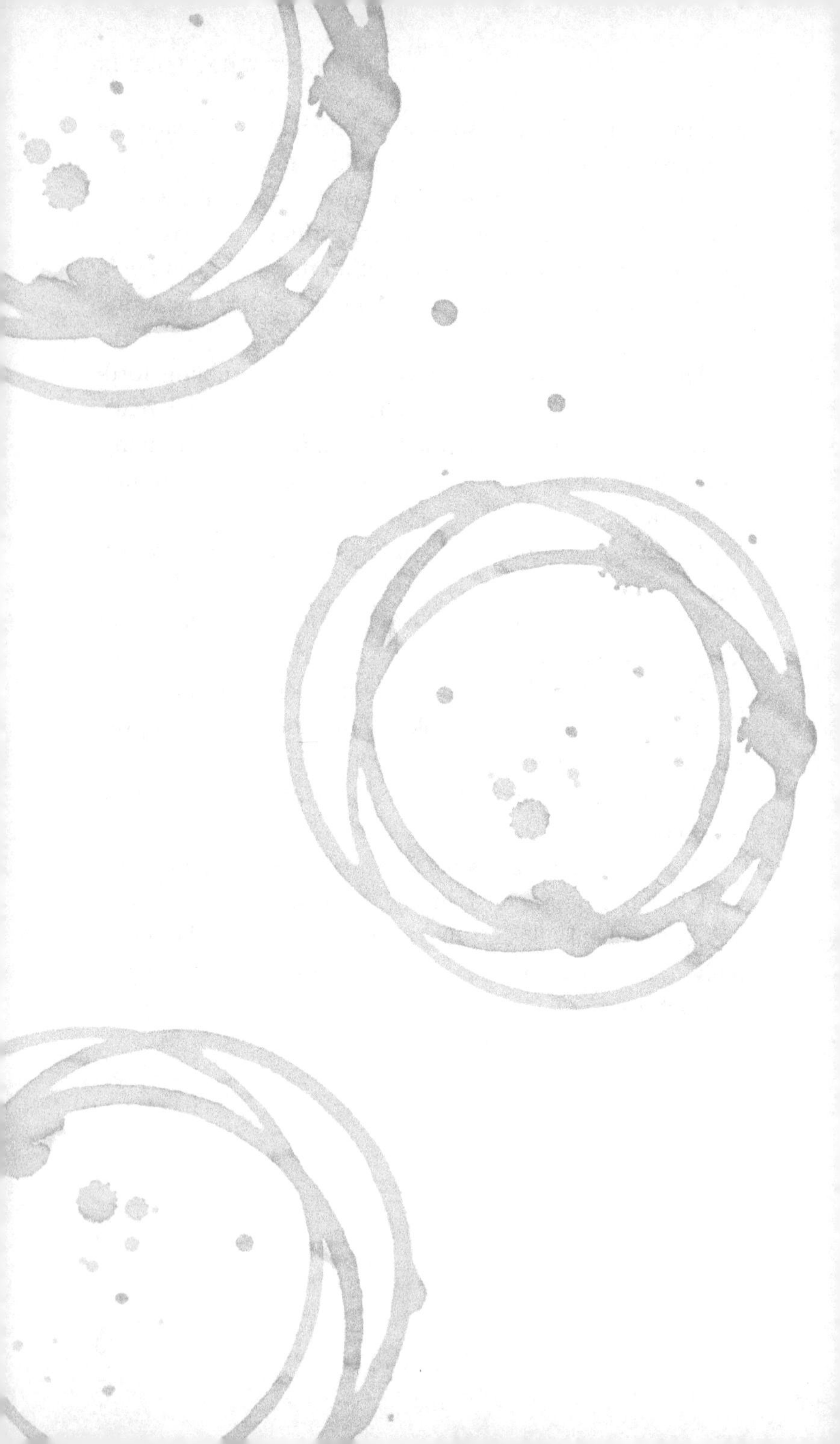

CHAPTER THREE

After the chaos of the afternoon rush dies down, I make my way toward the small employee bathroom. Once inside, I lean against the wall and take a few deep breaths. I don't understand why I feel overwhelmed during this time of the day. Scarlett tells me I should speak to a professional, but the idea of a therapist does not appeal to me. I'd rather deal with my feelings at home all by myself. When in the company of others, I put on a fake smile and act happy. I set a personal rule to not let my dad's negativity affect my day, but I don't always follow it. In reality, my actions don't always match my words.

I've always had this knack for switching my mood from negative to positive in an instant, just like flipping a light switch. Over the years, I've learned to distract myself whenever something bad happens. Whether it's binge-watching TV, getting lost in a good book, or throwing myself into work, it's become a habit. Whenever negativity creeps into my life—even if it isn't about my dad—I securely confine it within the chambers of my mind, sealing it away in a deeply buried box. But sometimes the lock doesn't hold.

I take a deep breath, wash my hands, and then dry them.

The aroma of freshly brewed coffee envelops me as I survey the counter, mentally taking stock of the tantalizing food items on display. This café, my sanctuary, holds my dreams and aspirations.

Glancing at the clock, I'm hit with an idea. I turn to Scarlett, who's diligently wiping down the tables. "Hey, Scar," I call out. "Wanna have a movie night at my place?"

Scarlett's eyes light up with excitement. "Hell yeah! Count me in. Let's head there right after we close."

A smile plays on my lips as a memory dances in my mind. "Remember that time we hit the beach, and a crab made itself comfortable on my butt? I freaked out, screamed like a banshee, and ran as if my life depended on it!"

Scarlett bursts into infectious laughter as she pulls out her phone at lightning speed and searches for the video she captured that day. "Oh my god, Hailey, that was epic!" Her eyes shine with glee. "I've got the evidence right here!"

"Oh, my gosh!" I exclaim.

Scarlett shakes her head, her smile fading to a frown. "That day didn't have the best ending. Visiting his grave is still unreal to me," she says.

As I look at her, I recall the memory of his accident.

Scarlett's phone suddenly rang with a shrill tone, jolting us from our conversation. "Mommy" flashes across her screen.

"Hello," she greeted, but soon the color drains from her face, her eyes widening in fear.

Scarlett's voice trembled as she spoke into the phone, "What? What happened? Is he okay?" Her grip on the phone tightened, and I could see the fear in her eyes. "Joey was in an accident," she mouthed to me.

I raised my brows. "What hospital is he heading to?" I asked.

She repeated that question to her mom.

"The one across town," she explained.

"Let's go."

Without a second thought, we abandoned our half-drunk coffees and rushed to her car. As we sped through the streets, the world outside became a blurry, chaotic mess. Fear gripped our hearts, and the minutes seemed to stretch on endlessly.

Finally, we arrived at the hospital, our footsteps echoing through the sterile, white hallways. We found Joseph's room, and there he was. Life hung in the balance, like a fragile thread ready to snap.

The doctor, dressed in a sterile white coat, delivered the devastating news with a solemn expression. Joseph hadn't made it. Scarlett collapsed into a nearby chair, tears streaming down her face. I held her hand tightly, unable to find the words to comfort her.

We clung to each other. It was a moment when life changed forever, a reality that weighed heavily on our hearts.

WE KNEW WE WOULD ALWAYS CARRY THE WEIGHT OF THAT sorrow with us, a constant reminder of the day when the world turned gray and our lives were irrevocably altered. In the midst of our grief, we held onto each other, finding strength in our friendship as we navigated the overwhelming sadness that had become an indelible part of our lives. "Your brother would be incredibly proud of the woman you've blossomed into today," I say.

"Do you really think so?" she asks.

"I don't just think so, I know so." I give her a hug, "Now go finish your dishes."

"Uh, last time I checked, I'm your boss."

"But you're also my closest friend, and you care about me." I pout.

She responds with an exaggerated eye roll, then playfully extends her middle finger before striding into the kitchen.

I NESTLE INTO THE PLUSH COUCH, DRAWN INTO THE captivating world of the vampire movie we are watching. Scarlett sits beside me, her eyes glued to the screen as we dissect every scene, craving more romance and fewer mindless conversations between the characters.

The room reverberates with our laughter, filling the air with contagious energy. "Jacob and Bella deserve a love story that ignites hearts," I say, my voice filled with passion and frustration at the missed opportunities.

Scarlett's gaze shifts from the screen to me, and her lips curl into a knowing smile. "Alright, Hailey, spill the tea. What's the deal with Eric? That mysterious man who's been gracing the café with his presence. I can tell there's more to it."

I wave off her inquiry, trying to play it cool. "Oh, it's nothing, really. Just a couple of chance encounters. I hardly know him."

A playful glint dances in Scarlett's eyes as she leans in

and says in a flirtatious voice, "Honey, trust me. He wants more than just a friendly dinner. You've caught his eye."

"Oh, you heard him asking?" I chuckle, a mix of excitement and apprehension swirling within me. "Well, we'll see about that, but right now, I'm not sure if I'm ready for a relationship."

Scarlett gently rests a hand on my arm. "Sometimes, a little distraction can be just what you need. Give it a chance. It might surprise you."

My mind is clouded with doubts, yet, the allure of the unknown tugs at my heartstrings. We turn our attention back to the TV, surrendering to the mesmerizing vampire drama until exhaustion consumes us. We find comfort on my couch, but I can't get what Scarlett said out of my mind.

Eventually, I doze off to thoughts of how interesting it would be to go out with Eric.

CHAPTER FOUR

The morning sun peeks through the blinds, casting a soft glow on the room. As I stretch and yawn, memories of last night's vampire-infused marathon flood my mind.

Scarlett stirs beside me, her sleepy eyes meeting mine. "Did we really fall asleep watching *Twilight*?" she mumbles.

I laugh. "We sure did. It's a good thing we didn't wake up craving blood," I tease, playfully nudging her.

Scarlett chuckles. "Well, I can't make any promises about the blood cravings," she says with a mischievous glint in her eyes. "After all, you know how captivating those vampire stories can be."

I raise an eyebrow, feigning disbelief. "Oh, so you're secretly a vampire, huh? I guess I'll have to keep an eye on you," I reply, a mock seriousness in my tone.

"Better keep that garlic around!" she says.

I laugh and get out of bed. "I need to shower. You good here, or do you wanna go home?"

"I need to go home and feed my cat before she goes crazy."

"I hope you realize we used my car to get here."

"Yes, and my house is only half a mile away. I'll be fine."

"Okay, see you at work tomorrow," I say.

Scarlett grabs her phone and gets up from the couch.

"See ya," she responds, walking out the front door.

I decide to start my day with a hot shower. As the steam envelops the bathroom, I step under the warm water, allowing it to wash away the remnants of sleep from my body. The droplets massage my scalp as I lather my hair with apple-scented shampoo. As I scrub my skin with body wash, my thoughts wander to Eric. He had asked me out to dinner, and although part of me was excited, another part was filled with apprehension. I'm not sure I'm ready for a new relationship. I'm afraid of opening myself up to the possibility of love.

I let my mind drift as I cleanse away the doubt and fear, allowing the steamy warmth to surround me. With each passing moment, I feel a sense of release, as if the water is washing away not just the physical grime but also the emotional baggage that weighs me down.

Stepping out of the shower, I wrap a towel around my body. I lean against the bathroom sink and gaze at my reflection in the foggy mirror. Droplets of water trickle down and distort the image. In this hazy state, I feel a renewed sense of clarity, as if the steam has whisked away the fog of my worries.

With a deep breath, I grasp the cool metal handle of the bathroom door and gently push it open, walking to my bedroom and into reality.

As I move toward my wardrobe, my fingers glide past the array of clothing options, seeking the comfort of my favorite jacket and leggings. I slip them on, enjoying the soft embrace of familiar fabric against my skin. I dry my unruly hair with the towel and hastily tie it back into a loose ponytail, letting a few strands frame my face.

With my walking shoes securely laced, I make my way to the front door with a surge of excitement coursing through my veins. The world outside beckons, ready to reveal its daily secrets. As I step out onto the front porch, the coolness of the morning greets me.

I head out to the park, where I take most of my morning strolls. Here, the only sounds that break the silence are the distant chirping of birds and the gentle rustle of leaves as the breeze flows through the trees. Each step forward carries me deeper into a state of meditative bliss, a rhythmic movement that aligns my body and mind with the awakening world around me.

And then, as if the universe had orchestrated our meeting, I spot him. Eric. The enigmatic man who had effortlessly walked into the café and left an indelible mark on my thoughts. He sits beneath the shade of a towering tree, his gaze focused on the pages of a notebook. A surge of emotion washes over me—one of curiosity, intrigue, and an inexplicable connection that defies rational explanation. My heart skips a beat as my feet hesitate before deciding to carry me closer to him.

With every step, anticipation builds, fueled by the magnetic pull drawing me toward him. I stand before him, my voice escaping in a gentle greeting, barely audible above the surrounding symphony of nature.

"Hi," I say.

Eric lifts his head and meets my gaze with a look of surprise and recognition. A warm smile spreads across his face. I take a small, instinctive step closer to Eric. My heart pounds with curiosity, eager to unravel the enigma that he embodies. "I noticed you sitting here, nose buried in a notebook. What brings you to this spot?" I ask.

Eric's smile broadens. "Nature has always been my sanctuary. I find comfort here. It's where inspiration flows freely, and the pages of my notebook come alive."

His words resonate deeply within me. Surprising myself, I ask, "May I sit with you?"

A genuine warmth illuminates Eric's eyes, "Please," he responds.

I smile and sit down next to him. The first couple of minutes are quiet like neither of us is sure what to say.

"So, how long have you been working at the café?" he asks, finally breaking the awkward silence.

"Six years. My friend Scarlett owns the café and wanted me to work with her."

"She owns it?"

"Yeah, her family is pretty wealthy and got her started with it."

"That's pretty neat," he says.

I nod.

"I'm sorry if I was too forward the other day."

I reassure him with a smile. "Truly, it's no problem at all."

Eric glances at me. "Sorry if it's weird to say, but I find that you have a fascinating aura about you. It's as if there's a story waiting to be told."

I pause for a moment and allow his observation to sink in. "You're perceptive," I say, a hint of vulnerability seeping into my voice. "There is indeed a story—one filled with twists and turns, triumphs, and heartaches. But it's not a story I often share."

His words touch a chord within me.

His eyes soften, and in that moment, I feel a sense of trust, something I don't feel often or this easily. "I suppose we're all shaped by our experiences," I begin tentatively. "And sometimes, it takes the right person to inspire us to share those experiences. I've always had a love for stories. They have a way of transporting us to different worlds, helping us understand ourselves and others. And yet, my story... well, it's been a bit of a journey."

"Mine too. Maybe one day we will be in a place to share our stories with each other."

"Maybe," I say with a smile. I look down at my phone and see the time. "I gotta head over to Scarlett's," I tell him, standing up.

"See you later?"

"Sure."

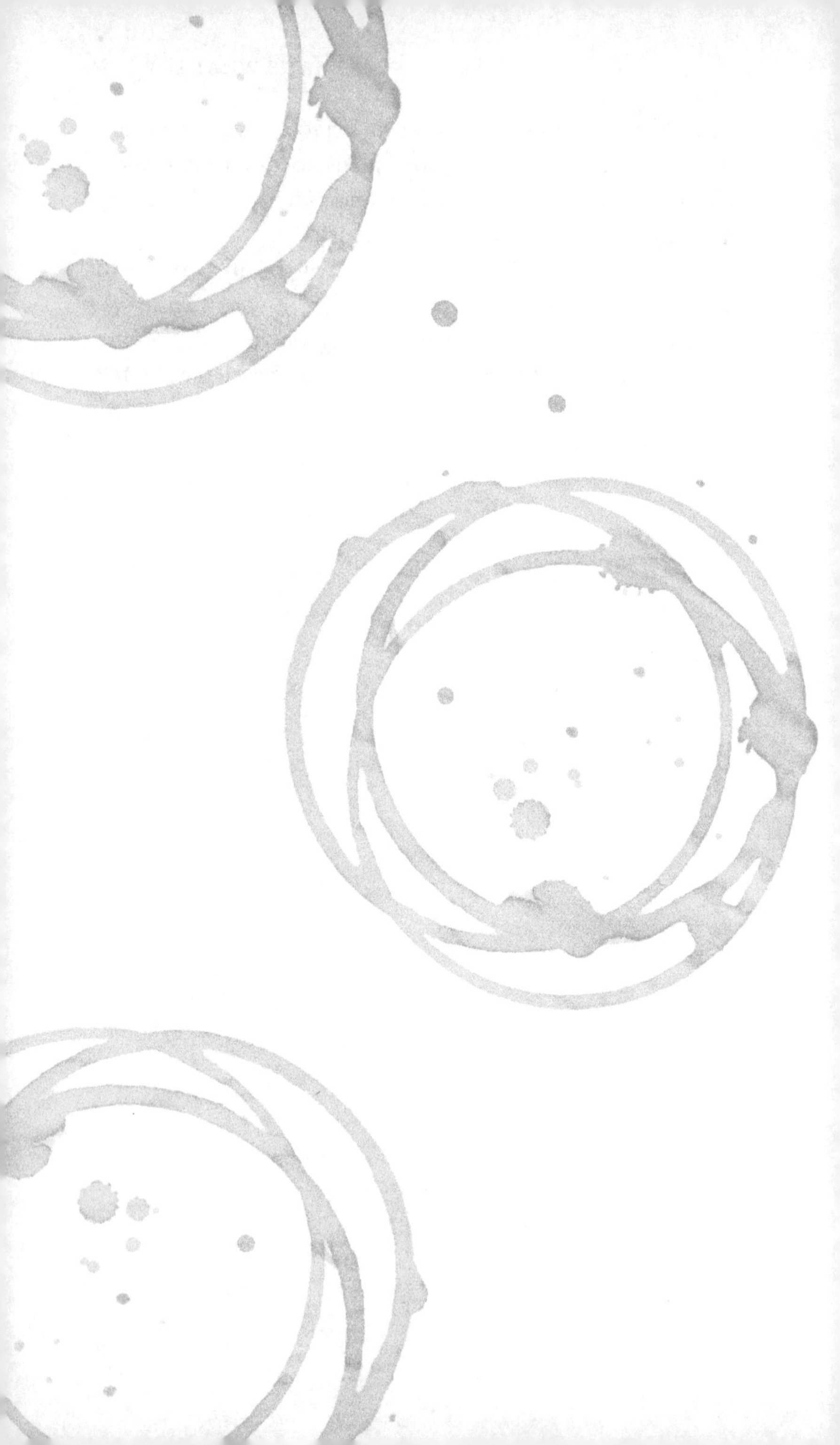

CHAPTER FIVE

THERE'S SOMETHING ABOUT ERIC AND HIS SMILE THAT warms my heart. Any time I am around him, he gives me butterflies, and my heart aches in a good way. I've never felt that before. With my last boyfriend, I never felt this way.

Once, my ex-boyfriend had let the words, "I love you" slip out while we were making out on the couch. It was the first time a guy, other than my dads, had said that to me. I wasn't sure if I loved him, but I brushed it aside and continued kissing him until he started trying to undress me. He was a kind enough, good-looking man, but I couldn't bring myself to want more from him after those three words. I left in a hurry, went straight home, and spent the entire night contemplating whether I should keep him around. I didn't even give him an explanation for why I left.

I never spoke to him again. Sometimes I wonder, did he truly love me? Did he genuinely want to be with me, or were those words just a means to an end? But these are questions I'll never know the answers to.

As I approach Scarlett's house, I see my mom's car parked in the driveway. I knock on the front door, and when Scarlett answers, she looks at me wide-eyed and motions toward the kitchen.

"My mom or Ray?" I mouth silently.

"Your mom," she whispers.

I look at her with furrowed brows. My mom doesn't stop by unannounced, ever. I step inside the house. As I make my way into the kitchen, I spot my mom sitting at the kitchen table.

"Mom?" I say, my voice filled with concern.

"Oh, Hailey! I swung by your house, but you weren't there, and you weren't answering your phone," she responds with a troubled expression.

"What's going on?" I ask, looking at my phone. I didn't even notice my phone going off.

"There's something wrong with your dad," she explains.

"Yeah, something has been wrong with him since before you two met," I respond with a tinge of bitterness.

She gives me a disapproving look before continuing. "No, I mean your other dad. Ray."

My heart skips a beat. "What?"

"He's not doing well, honey," she says, her voice filled with sadness.

"Mom, please, tell me what's going on." My voice cracks as I sit down next to her.

My mom fumbles with her fingers, her face reflecting worry and deep concern. "His cancer has made him weaker, and he's in the hospital."

I don't say anything for a moment.

"Honey?" My mom's voice breaks through my thoughts, bringing me back to the present. "Honey, I know it's hard to hear," she says softly, reaching out to hold my hand.

Tears well up in my eyes, but I blink them back, trying to stay strong. "How long does he have?" I ask, my voice trembling.

My mom takes a deep breath, her eyes filled with both pain and determination. "A few weeks, maybe," she reveals. "The doctors say there isn't anything they can do. They can only help him be more comfortable."

I nod, trying to absorb the information. "We have to be there for him, Mom. He's always been there for us."

She squeezes my hand gently and nods.

A mix of emotions courses through me—fear of what lies ahead, determination to support my dad, and a desire to reciprocate the love and support my parents have shown me.

Taking a deep breath, I wipe away a stray tear and stand up. "I don't think I can deal with this right now. Scar, can we go out tonight?" I ask.

Scarlett looks at me with a frown. "Sure."

"Hailey, please," my mom calls after me.

"Mom, I can't talk about this right now, please."

She looks at me, tears in her eyes, and nods.

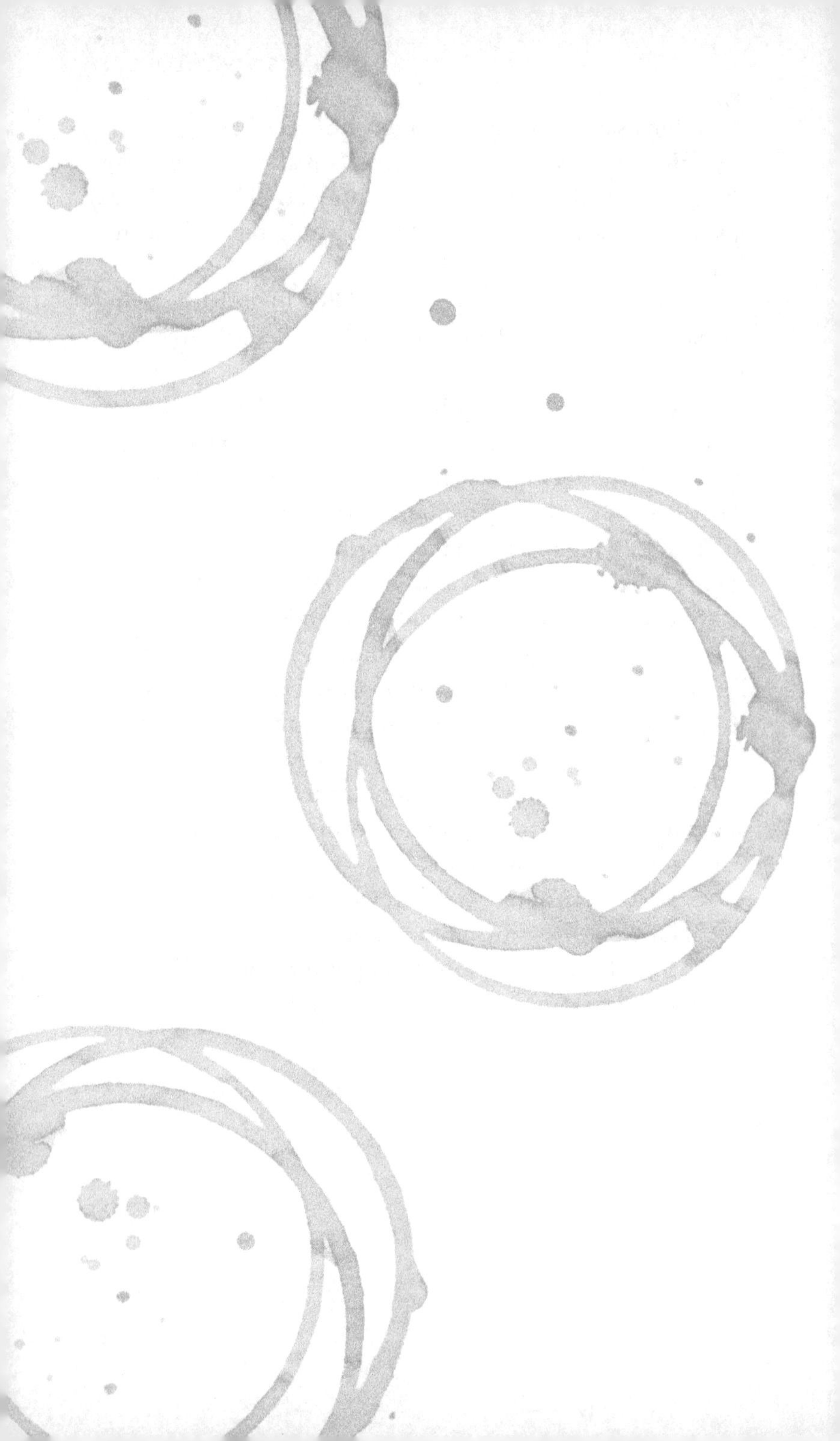

CHAPTER SIX

I STAGGER INTO THE HOUSE. THE NIGHT OUT WITH Scarlett helped to numb the pain, but I can still feel it bubbling below the surface. A mix of anger and pain still flows through me. It's hard to fathom the reality before me. The person who showed me genuine fatherly love is now slipping away from this world, and I feel powerless. My entire world is collapsing, and I'm struggling to process the gravity of this news.

I toss my phone onto the coffee table, lie on the couch, and close my eyes. What did I ever do to the world for it to go against me?

As I close my eyes and rest my head, I finally fall asleep.

MY PHONE PINGS AND WAKES ME UP. I ROLL OVER AND FACE the backside of the couch to avoid my phone when it pings again.

What the fuck. Frustrated, I flip back over and grab my phone from the coffee table.

DAD

Why won't you ever text me back?

Here we go again.

DAD

Hello? I'm your father!

Text me back!

I am saved from having to respond by a knock at my door. I sigh with relief and set my phone back on the table. As I make my way through the hallway, I see my mom through the window. She looks distraught. She walks in as I open the door and whips around to look at me. I close the door before facing her.

"Mom, what's wrong?"

"What's wrong? Where the hell were you last night?" she asks. Her face is puffy from crying.

"Scarlett and I went for drinks, remember?" I remind her as I walk past her and into the kitchen.

"Oh, that's right. I forgot. Well, your dad keeps asking why you aren't responding to his messages. I told him you were probably asleep."

"Which dad?" I scoff.

She rolls her eyes. "The one who helped make you."

I glance at her while I grab a glass of water. I don't get why he always contacts her if I don't respond. Can't he tell I'm ignoring him?

"Mom, he treats me like shit. I don't want to respond to him all the time."

"I'm not saying you have to." She crosses her arms and walks into the living room like she owns the place. I roll my eyes and follow her, sitting down next to her on the couch.

"You need more wall art or something. The place echoes."

"Buy me some then."

"You have a job, don't you?"

"Yeah, not enough money to get wall art. What am I supposed to do, use my looks?"

"If that's what it takes, then yeah." A smirk appears on her face.

"Mom!" I let out an exasperated chuckle. There was silence for a few moments. I know she's worried about Dad —the one who isn't my blood relative but treats me as his own. Her lip quivers as she fumbles with her jacket. "Mom?"

"Yes?"

"How are you doing?" I ask.

She looks up at me with a frown.

"Just trying to keep my head up."

I nod, unsure of what to say.

"Well, I'm going to head up to the hospital. Do you want to come with me?" she asks. Her eyes are bloodshot from her tears. I don't know how to face him without tears forcing themselves out like a reservoir breaking through its dam.

"I'll come by later. What room is he in?"

"Floor 7, room 204."

"Okay, I'll call you when I head over."

I stand up and offer her my hand. She takes my hand and stands up, pulling me into a hug. I wrap my arms around her, trying to keep the tears from breaking through.

"I love you, Momma."
"I love you, too."
She walks out of the front door, closing it behind her.
And that's when the tears come.

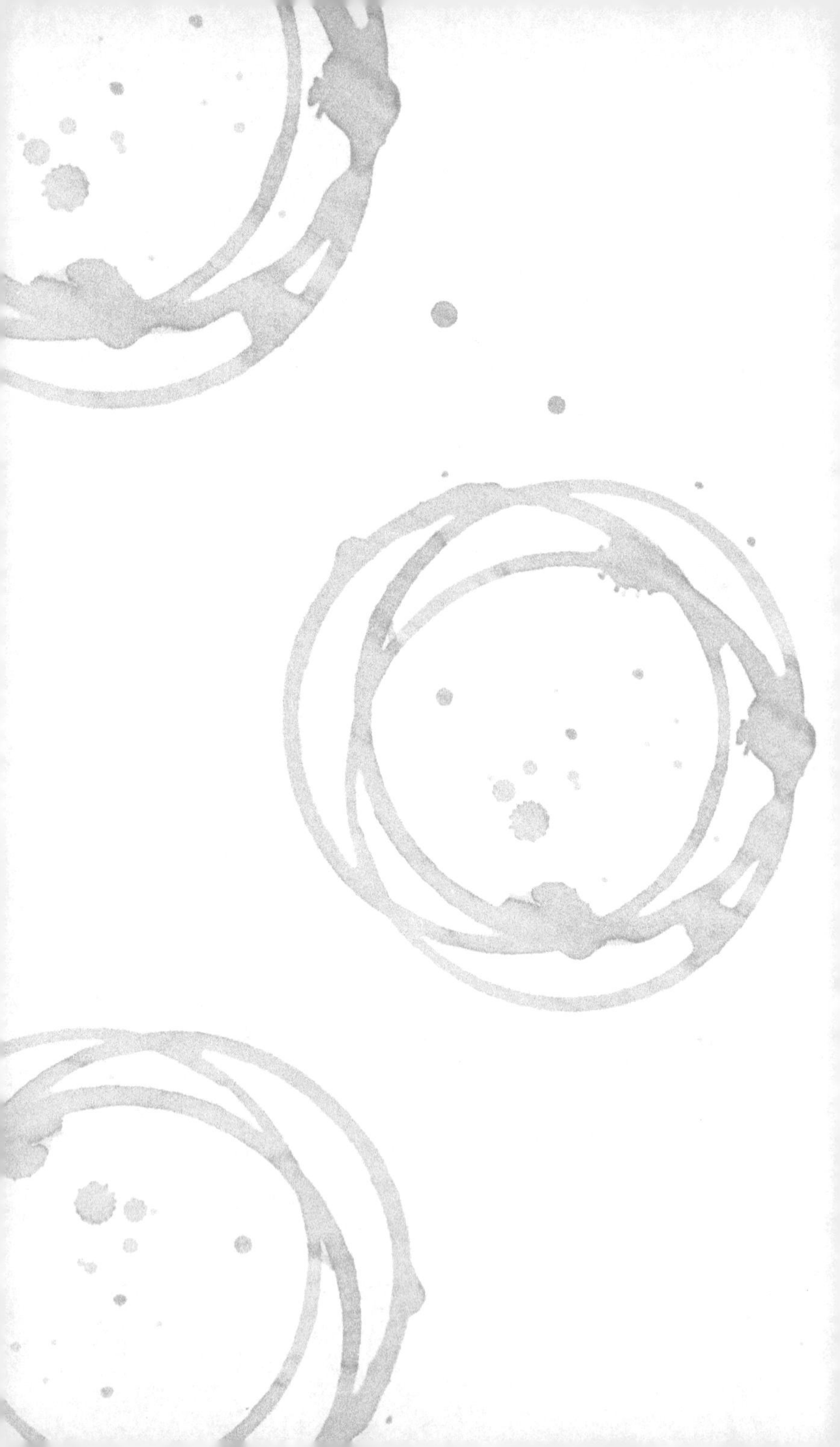

CHAPTER SEVEN

I reach for my phone and tap Scarlett's name. I press the call button with trembling fingers, desperate for her comfort. After a few agonizing rings, it goes to voicemail. *Damn it, she must be asleep.* I sigh in frustration, feeling the weight of the world crushing me. I step outside, lock the door behind me, and settle into my car.

A heavy sense of worry, discomfort, and pain presses upon my chest like an unforgiving brick. The wind blows through my hair as I drive away, offering a gentle warm breeze. But it does little to ease the burden I carry.

With the sun high above the ocean, casting a beautiful glistening light upon the waves, I try to find solace in this fleeting moment of tranquility. The chaos of my life momentarily fades away, and for a moment, I forget the turmoil that plagues me.

With the radio blaring catchy, upbeat pop music, I allow myself to let go. My hair flows freely, and I sing along, hoping to release some of the sadness that's been consuming me. Gradually, the drive to Scarlett's feels smoother, and a glimmer of hope flickers within. Oh, how I wish I could cling to this feeling forever—this sense of liberation and being free from the shackles of my troubles.

I pull into Scarlett's driveway and take a deep breath, hesitating for a moment before stepping out of the car. The weight on my chest seems to intensify as I approach her door.

With a knot in my stomach, I walk up to her front door and knock softly. No response. I knock again, this time a little louder. Still nothing. The silence is deafening, echoing my inner turmoil. I try calling her, hoping she'll answer. The phone rings, and my heart pounds in my chest with every passing second. Finally, I hear a faint sound coming from inside the house. Her footsteps.

Scarlett opens the door.

"Goodness, Scar, I was worried for a minute."

"Shhh," she says, gesturing for me to come inside.

I raise a brow and walk inside, immediately noticing men's clothing on the couch.

"Scar, who'd you bring home last night?"

Her eyes widen. "He hasn't left yet!"

"Who?" I ask while letting out a laugh.

"Zack, a new guy I met recently."

I plop myself on the couch, looking at her with a cheesy smile. I'm glad to see her forgetting about the coffee shop for a moment.

"Maybe you'd have some fun too if you let loose a little," she jokes, sitting next to me and placing her feet over the top of my legs.

"Nah, I enjoy being alone," I say.

Footsteps make their way down the stairs, and I look up to see Zack, dressed in only dark blue gym shorts.

"Oh, hi, Zack!" I stand up, and so does Scarlett.

"Hi, uh, Hailey, right?" he asks while reaching out his

hand. I smile and nod, shaking his hand. "Nice to meet you."

"Okay, so, see you later, Zack?" Scarlett asks.

"How about tomorrow? There's a party going on at my house. You can come too, Hailey," he offers.

"She'll be there," Scarlett says.

I look at her with wide eyes.

"Cool, bye, ladies," he says as he grabs his clothes and walks out the door, closing it behind him.

I look at her for a solid minute before sitting back down.

"Oh, come on, Hailey, he might have some single friends!"

"What part of 'I'm not ready' do you not understand? It's bad juju having someone in my life right now."

"Hailey, I'm not asking you to date, just mingle a bit, make some friends!" she explains.

I sigh. "Okay… I guess I'll go."

She squeals and grabs my arm, then drags me up the stairs.

I COULDN'T STOP THINKING ABOUT DAD, ABOUT HOW MUCH pain he must be in from the cancer. I didn't even know he was sick. Cancer is evil—fucking evil.

"Earth to Hailey!" Scarlett snaps her fingers in my face.

"I'm sorry," I apologize and shake my head. I rest my back against the foot of her bed. "I honestly have no words about anything right now."

Scar lays her dress down on the bed and sits crisscross in front of me. "Honey, I love you so much. I'm here for you. And I hate that this is happening. He's like a father to me, too." She reaches out and pulls me into a hug.

Crying out all of the pain into her shoulder, the tears fall, and I sound like I swallowed a squeaky toy, but I don't care. I need this. She hugs me tighter, and I can feel her breathing tighten up. She's also beginning to cry. Her crying makes me cry harder. Eventually, I pull away and look at her. Her blue eyes are bloodshot, probably just as much as mine. She wipes her face, and I do the same.

"Let's just forget about this. And go to work," she suggests.

I nod my head in agreement, then grab my purse and stand up.

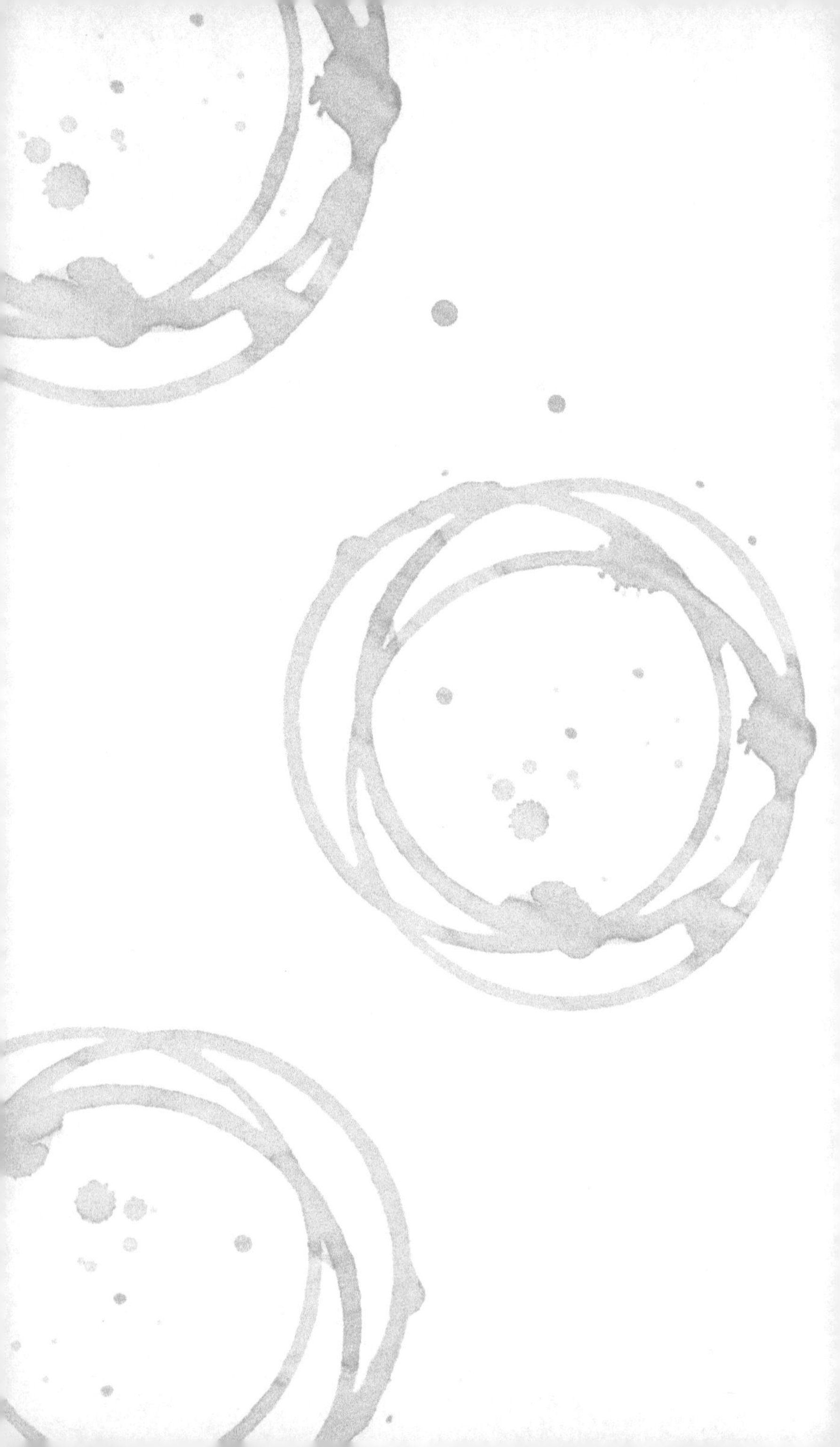

CHAPTER EIGHT

This evening is game night at the café. Everyone comes in and plays card games or board games. It's our small town's tradition. The whole town seems to be here tonight, and it's not even six yet. The night bears a cooler breeze than usual, and a storm is on the horizon. I've handed over the hosting reins to Scarlett this time. Tomorrow night is Zack's party, a decision I'm still wavering on. If I don't try to have some fun, I will probably just end up sitting in a corner, drowning in my thoughts. I just have to make it through today. Take it one day at a time.

Music pours from the speakers, infusing the room with an infectious energy. The tables are set with an array of board games, a variety at each table—chess, Sorry, Monopoly, and more—offering choices for everyone. The rule is simple: play something to partake in game night. And if you're done with one game, there's always another waiting for you.

"Alrighty, everyone, listen up!" Scarlett's voice commands attention as she stands atop the counter. "We're switching things up tonight," she says, pulling out a wad of cash. "The first table to conquer all five board games wins a $500 prize and free dinners for the rest of the summer!"

The crowd erupts in cheers and applause, and I chuckle, shaking my head with a fond smile.

"LET'S GO!" Scarlett's rallying cry ignites a frenzy of activity. Game choices are swiftly made, tables fill with players, and boards are set for action.

"We've never offered a reward before," I say.

"Yeah, but it's all about keeping the business thriving. More money, honey," Scarlett quips.

Laughing, I move behind the counter, wiping it down to prepare for tonight's rush. As I am finishing up, the doorbell's chime interrupts my focus, and I look up to find Eric entering with a small group.

"Hey, Hailey, room for three tonight?" His voice sparks a smile onto my lips.

"Absolutely, follow me." I grab three menus before heading to the dining area. I lay the menus on the table in the booth and take out my pen and pocket notebook while they are getting seated.

"What can I get y'all started with?" I ask.

"I'll have a Sprite," Eric says.

"Just coffee, no sugar," an older man says.

"Sprite for me as well, please," a younger guy chimes in.

"I'll get right on it." I note down the orders before making my way to the kitchen. I grab two tall glasses and a mug, then fill each with the requested beverages and return to the table.

"Here you go, folks. Have you decided on food yet?" I ask.

"We're good with drinks for the night," Eric replies, his

eyes lifting to meet mine, his smile ever so charming. With a casual sweep of his hand, he brushes his hair back.

I stand there for a moment, caught in his gaze, feeling a flutter in my chest that I can't quite explain. "Alright then, just let me know if you change your mind," I say, my voice slightly breathless as I tear my attention away to head back behind the counter.

As I busy myself with some tasks, double-checking the inventory, the lights flicker for a second before plunging the room into darkness. Murmurs and surprised gasps fill the air, and then, amidst the laughter, I hear Eric's voice.

"Well, it looks like we're in for a little adventure," he quips in a playful tone, his comforting words weaving through the dark like a thread.

"Yeah, game night just got a whole new level of challenge," I reply, my voice carrying amusement and curiosity.

Without hesitation, I pull my cell phone out and turn on its small flashlight. Turning around, I bump into something hard. A scent of cologne fills the surrounding air. I nearly fall over, but a firm set of hands place themselves on my hips, keeping me balanced. I shine a light into the eyes of the person holding onto me.

"Wow, girl, you trying to blind me?" Eric asks, laughing.

"I'm sorry!" I quickly face the light down.

"You okay?"

His hands are still on my hips. I look down and feel warmth rushing to my cheeks. He notices and takes them off. "Just didn't want you to fall." He scratches the back of his head, and I can sense the nervousness in his voice.

"It's alright." I clear my throat. As I look up at him, I can feel butterflies fluttering inside my stomach. "Would you help me grab candles in the back?" I ask.

"Uh, yeah, sure." He follows me as conversations continue behind us in hushed tones.

Scarlett gives me a thumbs-up with a cheeky smile, and I roll my eyes. I give a subtle nod as Eric and I both slip away from the crowd, making our way to the small office at the rear of the building. "Ah, here they are," I say, pointing toward a box of candles nestled high on a shelf among the clutter. He's right behind me now, his fingers stretching out, a gentle warmth brushing my skin as he reaches for them. His breath, oh so warm, tickles my ear, and it's like a thousand tiny sparks igniting inside me. Goosebumps surge across my body, and I can't help but shiver.

He lays the box down on the desk with a quiet thud, and then his hands move to the drawers. I watch as he rummages through them, searching for matches. Each second feels like an eternity as I stand here on the edge of something thrilling, my heart pounding and my senses alive with the anticipation of what's to come.

I walk into the storage closet to retrieve a couple of holders—and to put a little distance between Eric and myself before I do something I'm not ready for.

When I return, Eric has already arranged a few candles in a rustic basket, ready to be carried out to the tables.

"We should have enough for each table," I say.

He looks at all the candles we have. "Agreed."

"Let's bring some light and charm to these tables," I say.

We set about our task, carefully placing candles at each table, watching as the flames cast a warm, inviting glow. The soft illumination dances across the faces of the guests, lending an air of intimacy to the scene. Eric and I exchange coy glances here and there while setting the candles down on tables and ledges.

I stop at the counter after I'm done, and Eric walks up to me with his hands inside his front pockets.

"Hailey, you sure know how to light up a room," he says with a shy smile.

I smile back, also shyly, feeling a mixture of nerves and excitement. "Thank you, Eric."

He nods and walks back to his table. Scarlett walks toward me with a smile. I catch Eric's eyes lingering on me for a moment longer. Scarlett nudges me, her playful expression saying it all.

"See, Hailey? Sometimes, all it takes is a little light to illuminate the possibilities."

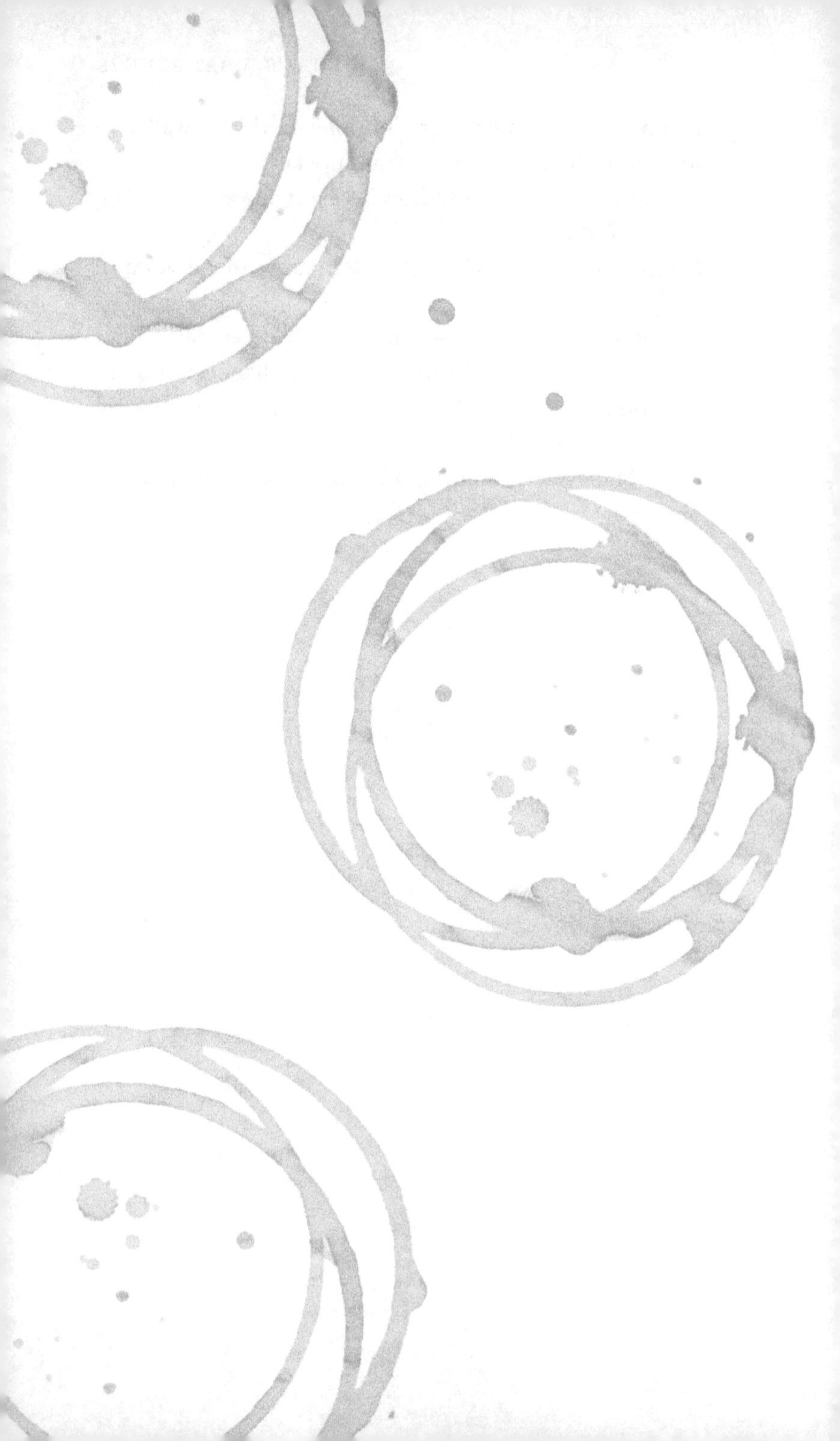

CHAPTER NINE

CANDLES FLICKER, CASTING A SOFT, DANCING GLOW AROUND the café as the power outage encompasses us. Thunder rumbles outside, and my fingers twitch involuntarily. *I hate storms.* Scarlett, a beacon of vibrancy in the dimness, moves gracefully, trying to keep the atmosphere alive despite the storm's intrusion.

Game night progresses under the candlelight until suddenly the lights flicker back on, taking us all by surprise. Cheers and applause erupt around us, and Scarlett's voice rises above the commotion. "We've got a winner for tonight's games!" All eyes are on the middle table, and Scarlett's mischievous grin makes me smile.

"Congratulations! You guys are the champions tonight! Enjoy your $500 prize and free dinners for the summer!" She hands a couple a written check, along with a certificate for the café. The couple yells in excitement. I notice some disappointed faces, but they are still cheering for the winners.

I walk behind the counter and grab my phone from my pocket. There is a missed call from my mom and four missed texts from my dad. My shaky thumb hovers over the messages from him. I click it open and let out a shaky breath.

DAD

I have tried reaching out, yet you never respond. Why is that?

I'm your dad, always will be!

I will sell all of my baseball cards just to pay the child support. I am sick of this shit!

You're a bitch, just like your mother!

I drop my phone on the counter. Teardrops gather and create their salty path down my cheeks. A hushed sob escapes my lips, an involuntary release of the heaviness clutching at my chest.

The sound of someone clearing their throat startles me. With a swift motion, I wipe my face, erasing any tell-tale signs of vulnerability. Eric stands before me. A surge of dread rushes through me, an instinctual recoil from the thought of anyone—especially him—bearing witness to my exposed fragility.

"Are you… okay?" His voice wavers slightly. He hands my phone back to me and our hands touch.

I manage a shaky smile. "Yeah, I'm… I'm fine," I respond, my tone a tad too dismissive. My heart races, conflicted between wanting to lean on him and being too stubborn to expose my pain.

He takes a step closer, his eyes searching mine as if attempting to decipher the truth behind my facade. "You don't seem fine," he says. "We've only known each other for a few days, but… I can tell something's wrong."

The sincerity in his words softens the walls I've built.

"It's just… family stuff," I admit with reluctance.

Eric nods slowly, his gaze unwavering. "I-I understand if you don't want to talk about it," he replies with a stutter. His vulnerability in communication is oddly endearing, and it somehow eases my apprehension.

I whisper, "Thank you," meeting his gaze that feels almost electric. Despite myself, I feel drawn to him, like our shared moments over the past few days have forged a connection stronger than mere acquaintanceship.

He seems so good, but it's too early. Stop it, Hailey.

His gaze holds mine, his concern unwavering. "If you ever want to talk, or even if you just need a distraction, I'm here," he tells me.

I nod, appreciating his sincerity and the refuge he seems to represent. "I might take you up on that one day." The tension in my shoulders eases ever so slightly.

He nods with a smile and walks back to his table.

THE STORM CALMS DOWN, THE RAINDROPS TURNING FROM fierce taps to gentle patters on the windowpane. Inside the café, the atmosphere shifts, too. The wild excitement that had filled the place during the power outage mellows into a calm buzz of contentment.

I look around the café and notice people getting up from their seats. As they all walk past me with smiles on their faces, I can't help but feel alone in this world. Everyone seems to have someone. I have my best friend, my mom, and my stepdad, but what about love? Scarlett keeps saying I need to try it out, but any time I try, my anger or jealousy problems cause issues, or I pull away because I know that getting close to someone also means heartbreak.

My perspective on love would probably be different if it weren't for the way my dad treats me. It's clear to me that many of my issues stem from his behavior; I'm not blind to that fact. If he belittles me the way he does, how can I possibly trust another man to be any different?

There have been many nights when I've struggled with the decision of whether to contact him or not during our months of not speaking. I wonder if trying to bridge the gap that seems to widen with each hurtful word he utters is better than the silence. While I understand that talking to him may not be the wisest decision, I can't help but wonder—he is my dad, after all. Scarlett has suggested I cut ties and sever the toxic connection that's been poisoning my self-worth for years. I've seen those memes about "cutting out negativity" and "surrounding yourself with positive vibes only," and part of me yearns for the simplicity of that solution.

But I can't help it. Despite everything he's done, despite the pain he's caused, there's still a part of me that holds on to the memory of the man he used to be. The one who played catch with me in the backyard, the one who cheered for me at school events. That version of my dad that made me feel loved and protected is the reason I can't just shut him out completely. Most of the good memories we have together were when he was on medication. The medication helped him be a better husband to my mom and a better dad to me. But after only a few months, he stopped taking the meds. To this day, I am still unsure of why.

I've grown stronger over the years, despite his attempts to tear me down. It's like my heart is engaged in a constant game of tug-of-war. On one side, there's the logical part of me that understands keeping my distance from him is essential for my mental health. On the other side, I feel the urge to be close to him. So, I find myself caught in this ongoing dilemma. Wanting to stand up for myself, to finally confront him about the damage he's done. Yet also hoping for some form of redemption, a glimmer of the dad I remember. My heart refuses to let go completely, even though my head tells me it's for the best.

As I reflect on all of this, I realize that maybe the storm outside is a metaphor for the storm raging within me. The flashes of lightning representing the moments of anger and frustration, the thunder echoing the pain he's caused. But then there's the rain, the cleansing force that can wash away the dirt and make way for fresh growth. I can't help but wonder if I can cleanse my heart, to let go of the pain while still holding onto the love I once felt.

"Hailey?" That soft but deep voice awakens me from my thoughts.

"Yes?" I respond, my attention shifting to Eric as he approaches again. His hands are tucked casually into his front pockets.

"Tonight was fun, despite the crazy storm," he says, a warm smile on his lips. "Scarlett really knows how to make people enjoy themselves, even if it's just with board games."

His words carry a lightness that I respond to, a welcome distraction from the heavy emotions that have been swirling within me. It's strange how easy it is to talk to him, how his presence seems to create a sense of comfort.

"It's like she turned the power outage into an unexpected adventure," I reply, a small smile tugging at the corner of my lips.

Eric nods, his eyes holding mine for a moment before he glances out the window at the retreating storm. "Sometimes it's in those unexpected moments that you find the most joy."

As his words hang in the air, I feel a warmth spreading through my chest, and a smile breaks across my face. "I couldn't agree more," I say as I nod. The storm outside has calmed significantly, and the soft patter of rain against the windows provides a soothing backdrop to our conversation.

As we walk toward the front door, I can't help but feel a mixture of emotions swirling within me. The connection I've felt with Eric is undeniable, and it's both exciting and nerve-wracking. I can't help but let out a sigh. My mind races, torn between the urge to protect myself and the longing for a connection.

I meet his gaze, my eyes holding his for a moment that feels like an eternity. "Eric, you know… I've been through a lot," I admit, my voice tinged with vulnerability. "And I'm not sure if I'm ready to open up to someone new. But" I trail off, the weight of my thoughts hanging in the air between us.

He nods slowly, his expression understanding. "I get it, Hailey. I don't want to rush you into anything you're not ready for."

There's a genuine sincerity in his words, and it's both comforting and terrifying. Part of me wants to take that step, to let myself feel something again. But the scars of the past are still tender, a reminder of the pain I've endured.

I reach into my pocket and pull out my phone, hesitating for a moment before handing it to him. "Give me your number?" I ask softly, hope and caution in my voice. "Just… give me some time, okay?"

He takes my phone with a nod, his fingers brushing against mine briefly, sending a shiver down my spine. "Of course," he replies, his voice steady. "We can go at whatever pace you like. Even if it's only as friends."

As he enters his number into my phone, a palpable wave of anticipation and excitement surges through me, tingling in every nerve.

He hands my phone back, and I notice a subtle shift in his demeanor. As he takes a step closer, leaning down to whisper in my ear, my heart races with anticipation. "Text me when you're ready," he murmurs, his breath brushing against my skin, igniting a complex cocktail of emotions within me.

His breath, warm and tingling, feels both tantalizing and oddly comforting. It carries a hint of seduction that sends a thrilling shiver down my spine. I can't deny the excitement bubbling within me, a potent mix of desire and intrigue. This pivotal moment, though seemingly anticlimactic on the surface, leaves me teetering on the precipice of something entirely new and electrifying. "Looking forward to it," I reply as he pulls back to look in my eyes. My heart flutters as our connection lingers.

As he leaves, I close the door behind him and turn the lock. I lean against it for a moment, letting out a deep breath. The café is now quiet. As I reflect on the evening's events, I can't help but marvel at the unexpected turn my night took.

"So, Hailey, spill the tea. How are things going with Eric?" Scarlett walks over from the dining area and asks.

I shoot her a look, feeling my cheeks flush with heat. "Seriously?"

"What? You're finally mingling again! I've been waiting for this!" she laughs.

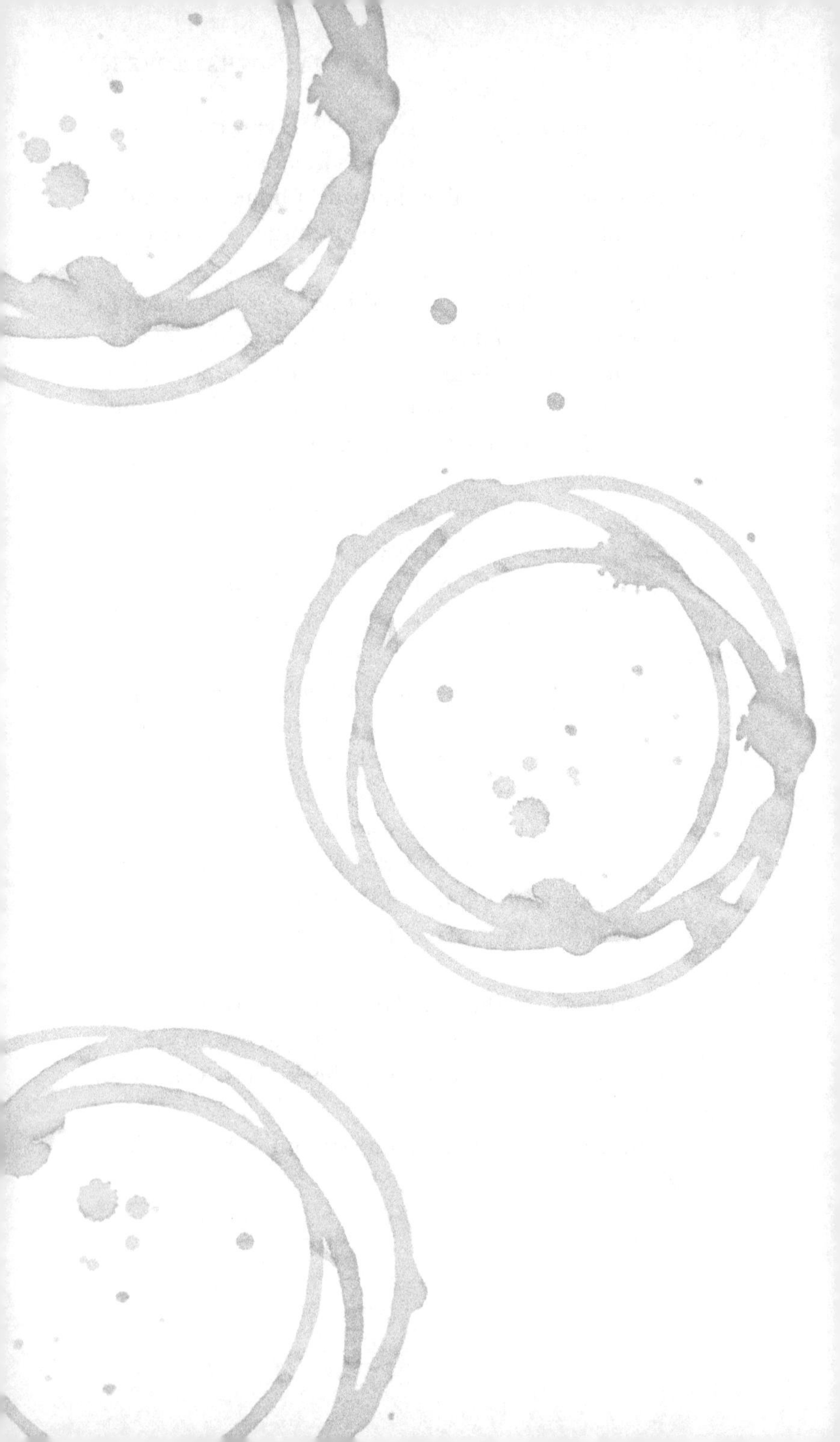

CHAPTER TEN

As I stand by the hospital window, watching the Monday morning sun cast long shadows across the parking lot, my thoughts are a tangled mess. Two days have gone by since Eric gave me his number, but I haven't sent a single text.

Turning away from the window, I walk back to my stepdad's room. Tubes and machines surround him; a constant reminder of the battle he's fighting. His eyes light up as he sees me enter, his pale face breaking into a faint smile. "Hey there, Hails," he rasps.

"Hey, Dad," I reply, trying to sound cheerful despite the lump in my throat. I pull up a chair and sit by his bedside, holding his hand. His grip is weak, but his spirit remains strong.

"So, tell me, what's been keeping you busy these past couple of days?" he asks, a mischievous glint in his eyes. He's always had a knack for reading my emotions, even when I tried to hide them.

I sigh, guilt and exhaustion washing over me. "Just

visiting you. You know, making sure you're not causing too much trouble for the nurses."

He chuckles, a raspy, breathy sound that somehow is infectious. "Well, you tell those nurses that I'm just adding a bit of excitement to their day."

We share a laugh, the tension in the room momentarily lifting. Ray has always been the one to find humor in the darkest moments. It is his way of coping, and I admire him for it. But beneath the jokes and the bravado, I can see the pain in his eyes, the worry he is trying to shield me from.

When my cell phone rings, I pull it out of my purse and walk out of the room, shutting the door behind me.

"Mom?" I ask.

"Hey sweetie, I'm heading over to the hospital now. Do you want me to stop by your place first and bring food?"

"I'm actually at the hospital. Can you bring it here, please?"

"Sure, babe! What would you like to eat?" I can hear her car's turn signal ticking in the background.

"Just grab a couple cheeseburgers, please,"

"Sure thing! Love you!"

"Love you, too." I smile and hang the phone up.

Back in the room, Ray is dozing off, his breathing steady. I pull my chair closer to him and take his hand once more.

While waiting for Mom, I decide to scroll through social media for a bit. Everyone is commenting on a post I made wishing Ray well, sending prayers, etc. Many friends and family members are heartbroken that he's leaving this world. I force my tears back more easily these days. Growing up and being talked to like shit by your own blood father makes you feel stronger.

I hear a knock on the door and turn around to see mom peeking through, a McDonald's bag in hand.

I widen my eyes, reach out, and open and close my hands with a cheeky smile on my face. "Gimmie!" I say. My mom laughs as she gives me the bag. I tear open the wrapper and take large bites in quick succession.

"Damn girl, you're gonna get a stomachache the way you eat," I hear Ray say, his voice breaking the silence of the room. I look over and see his eyes still closed, a playful grin tugging at his lips.

I chuckle softly, shaking my head. "You're just jealous that I found the hospital's secret stash of snacks."

"That's not hospital food," Ray lets out a weak laugh, his eyelids fluttering open. His gaze meets mine, and even though his body is weakened, I'm glad to see he can still make jokes. "You know, you're not getting out of dad jokes that easily."

I raise an eyebrow, a mock-serious expression on my face. "Oh, so you're saying I should start collecting my own stash of cheesy one-liners to fire back?"

He grins weakly. "Wouldn't dream of it, Hails."

Just then, my mom walks over to his other side, her presence bringing a sense of comfort and warmth. "Hi, honey," she says softly, her eyes reflecting a combination of weariness and relief.

"Took you long enough," Ray says, his smile growing wider. Despite the pain and the hospital gown, his charm and wit never seem to dim.

My mom chuckles, her fingers gently brushing his cheek. "You know me, always fashionably late."

Ray winks, a glimmer of his old self shining through. "Well, I suppose I'll forgive you this time."

"Get a room, you two," I laugh.

"I have one already."

I roll my eyes and smirk.

As I sit on my couch hours after visiting Ray, I wonder about my future wedding. Will I ever have one? What will it look like? The only man worthy enough to walk me down the aisle is dying and there's nothing I can do about it. Either I never marry, or I walk down the aisle by myself, a beautiful bouquet of roses in my hands, face guaranteed to be bright red from embarrassment. I don't care about the spotlight. My body shakes so much when I am nervous. I chuckle, thinking about how I might fall on my face before I reach the altar.

The TV is casting light through my dark living room and I sigh while trying to pick something to watch. I have work in the morning, so I should be going to bed instead of flicking through channels. I grab my phone and look through it. Photos from Zack's party on Saturday pop up on my social media feed. As I scroll through the photos, I think I see Eric in some of them and wonder if I should have gone to the party after all. I had decided to skip out because I wasn't feeling up for it.

Scarlett is aware of my difficult situation, but I don't expect her to be with me every moment. I want her to have a good time. I sigh, locking the screen and turning the TV off before making my way toward my bedroom. I plug my phone in and get cozy underneath my blankets, dozing off into dreamland.

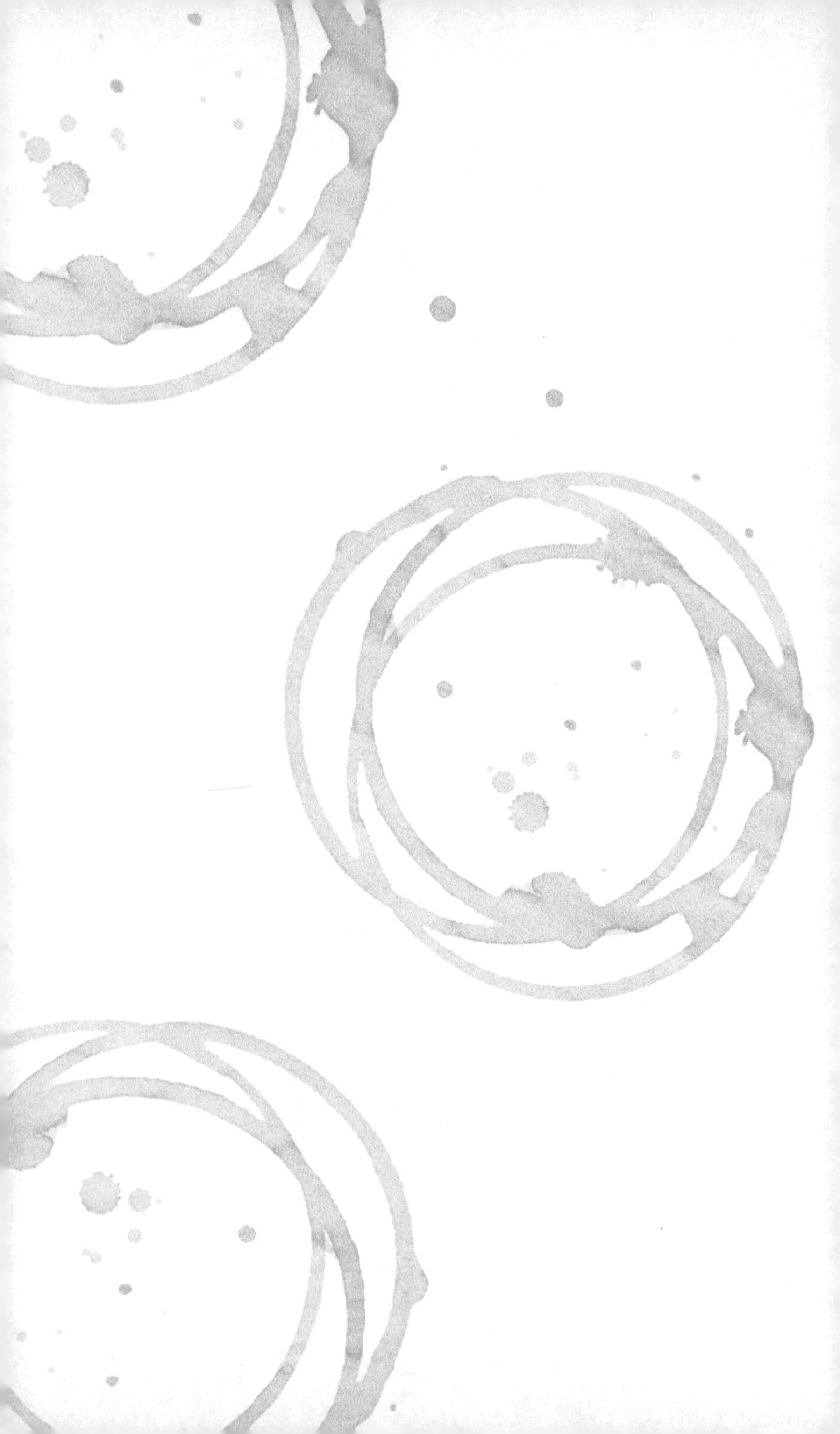

CHAPTER ELEVEN

THE FRIDAY MORNING RUSH DEMANDS MY FULL ATTENTION as I craft lattes and cappuccinos, each drink a canvas for my artistic touch. Amidst the steaming milk and espresso shots, Eric's image keeps surfacing in my thoughts. I wonder when I'll see him again.

Finally, the initial wave of customers subsides, allowing me a moment to wipe down the counter and adjust the display of freshly baked pastries. Glancing around, I notice the café's vibrant atmosphere—couples huddled over tables, friends catching up, and individuals engrossed in their own worlds.

With a quick glance at my phone, I see a text from Eric.

ERIC

Hey, hope you're having a great day. Would love to catch up sometime soon.

The words swirl in my mind, but before I can muster the courage to type them out, Scarlett appears by the counter.

"You look like you're lost in thought," she teases with a knowing grin.

I smile back, attempting to hide my slight embarrassment. "Just thinking about today's specials and how much cinnamon goes into the latte art," I reply, my fingers lightly tapping on the counter.

Scarlett arches an eyebrow. "Cinnamon, huh? Is that what they're calling it these days?"

I chuckle, feeling a warmth creep into my cheeks. Scarlett has an uncanny knack for picking up on things. "You caught me," I admit, raising both of my hands up in defense.

"Uh-huh, sure. Well, if you ever need someone to spill the cinnamon with, I'm here."

"Thanks, I appreciate that."

She walks into the back, leaving me alone at the register.

I find myself staring at my phone again. Today seems like as good a day as any to send that text. My fingers finally start to dance across the screen, composing the message to Eric.

ME

I'd love too.

Just as I hit send, the café door chimes once more, and a wave of new customers stream in, breaking my focus.

Sighing, I put my phone back in my apron pocket, turning my attention to the customers lining up at the counter. The door chimes again and I look up and lock eyes with the man I was just thinking about. A jolt of energy runs through my body, and I take a deep breath.

Chill, Hailey, chill.

His turn to order finally comes, and he approaches the

counter. "Hi, Hailey! How are you doing?" he asks with a smile. "It looks very busy this morning."

I straighten my posture and chuckle. "Yeah, it's been a very busy morning."

He crosses his arms and I can't help but notice he cut his hair, less shaggy and more short sides and longer on the top.

"Could I order a coffee again with a muffin?" he asks, his eyes sparkling with mischief.

"Of course," I reply, a smile tugging at the corners of my lips. "Black like last time, right?"

He leans in a little closer. "You've got an excellent memory." His wink sends a delightful shiver down my spine.

"To go or for here?" I ask.

His gaze lingers on mine for a moment, and then he answers, his voice lower and more seductive, "Oh, umm, could I get it to go? I have a goodbye party later tonight for my friend Zack, and I need to help prepare the house for him."

I nod, stepping gracefully around the counter. My movements are deliberate, and I can't help but add a touch of allure as I pour his coffee into a to-go cup, expertly securing the lid. Placing the cup and muffin on the counter, I ring up his order.

Before I can announce the total, he surprises me by handing over a twenty-dollar bill with a sly grin. "Keep the change," he says, his voice dipped in suggestion. "I'll see you later?"

I nod, and he turns and walks out the door.

"Well, that was quick," Scarlett says as she walks up behind me.

"Are you ever going to stop sneaking up on me like that?" I ask.

"No. Also, did I hear him say Zack?"

"Yeah, why?"

"Because my Zack has the same party; he's moving out of town."

I look at her with eyes wide, "So they do know each other. I thought I saw him in pictures of the party last weekend."

"Looks like you are definitely going to a party with me this time. Now, finish up what you're doing. We have inventory to do, girly!"

Scarlett walks away, taking her gloves off and heading into the kitchen.

I might as well go to the party. There's only so many excuses I can use and I'm excited by the idea of seeing Eric again.

THE DAY HAS BEEN BUSY, BUT THE BUSIER WE ARE, THE faster the time goes by. Fridays are always crazy, though I'm not sure if it's because of Scarlett's freebie-muffin Friday or because the weekend is right around the corner. Probably a mix of both.

I feel a buzz from my pocket and pull out my phone. Then my heart drops to the pit of my stomach. I could almost puke.

"I have to see a doctor next week about my leg. They found a blood clot."

My dad texted me. This isn't the first time he has said something like this, so I'm never sure if it's the truth or a way to get me to respond to him.

"Keep me updated," I reply.

After about a minute of staring at my phone, hoping for a response, I realize it isn't coming. I place my phone back into my pocket and sigh. When will this cycle between him and me end? I grab the inventory list and begin marking down items. I love my job, but today, I cannot wait until I can clock out.

I punch my clock out code into the computer while Scarlett wipes down the tables. All the customers have already left.

"So, are we still going to his party?" I ask, walking toward her.

"Ah, eager now, are we?"

I can't help but smile as I roll my eyes, "Look, okay, you're right. I need to mingle more."

She places her rag over her shoulder and claps her hands. "Okay, then, let's go!" she says. "But we need to freshen up at my house first."

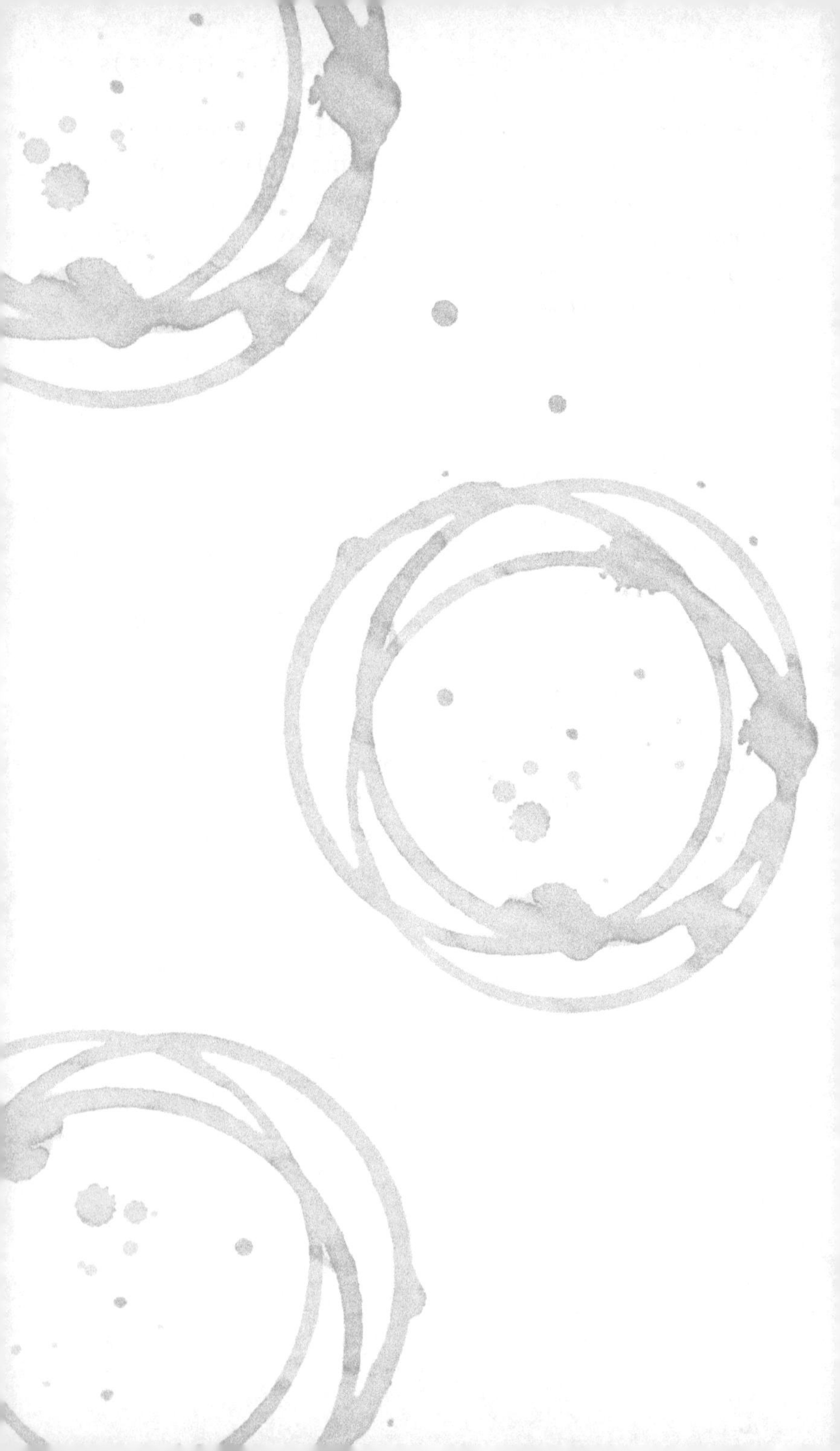

CHAPTER TWELVE

Dressed in white shorts and a black V-neck T-shirt, I slip into my white tennis shoes.

"You seriously need to quit abusing your shoes like that," Scarlett remarks with an edge.

I scoff. "And how's that?"

"Putting them on without untying them first? That's a shortcut to wrecking them," she says while tugging up her black leather boots.

I wave off her concern. "Relax."

"Your money, remember?"

"You're the one who's funding it," I shoot back, not one to be outdone.

"You've got a point there. Just take care of your stuff, you dork," she jabs, a smirk playing on her lips.

I chuckle and rise from my seat, giving my hair an exaggerated flip and checking myself out in the mirror.

"Ready to rock the party?" she asks.

"Can't say I'm overly enthusiastic."

As we step inside the waterfront house, the thumping music assaults my ears. The crowd swirls, and a riotous disco ball dangles overhead in a kaleidoscope of colors.

"Hey, Scarlett, Hailey!" Zack's voice cuts through the chaos as he greets us near the archway.

I muster a somewhat forced smile. "Hey."

After Scarlett and Zack share a hug, he turns to me. "Word is you're familiar with Eric."

Scarlett must've blabbed, or perhaps Eric's mentioning me. The latter seems unlikely.

"We've crossed paths, I guess." I shrug, exchanging a quick glance with Scarlett, who silently mouths an apology. "I'm thinking of exploring," I continue, needing a distraction from the tension.

"Need company?" Scarlett offers.

"Nah, I'll manage."

"Just give a shout if you change your mind," she offers before sauntering off with Zack.

"Sure thing!"

Stepping onto the patio, I'm greeted by a breathtaking sight. The porch and rails are adorned with shimmering fairy lights that cast a dreamy glow onto the water. Looking to escape the noise, I descend the steps and head toward the water's edge.

Seated upon the aging dock, my legs dangle over the edge, mirroring how my heart hangs heavily within me. The ocean's waves reflect my mind—a whirlwind of emotions all centering around my two dads. My stepdad's battle with cancer consumes my thoughts, a cruel reminder of his frailty and the gnawing fear that this ruthless disease will claim him. I wish so desperately he could be freed from this relentless torment—that his pain could cease and our lives could escape this constant shadow of suffering.

My biological father's presence haunts me, a bittersweet phantom lingering in my heart. I yearn for him to break free from his immaturity and be the father I crave. The ache to be truly seen and loved by him cuts deep—an unhealed wound. But I'm powerless over his actions.

As I stand by the water's edge, the serene landscape surrounding me, tears well up in my eyes. The gentle lapping of the water against the shore invites me to release my pent-up emotions. My face contorts with sadness, my breath quivering as I cry. Each tear that falls into the water carries a piece of my heartache, cleansing me of some of the pain.

The salty tears mix with the cool breeze, and for a moment, I let myself fully feel the weight of my longing and frustration.

Lost in the somber thoughts that bind me, a gentle tap on my shoulder yanks me back to reality. I turn to find Eric—the man I've "crossed paths" with—standing there. He gives a small smile and slides onto the dock, settling down next to me. The creak of the wood beneath us breaks the silence as he clears his throat.

"Can I sit here?" he asks, his voice surprisingly warm.

I nod, managing a small smile of my own. "Sure."

The silence settles, and I feel oddly comfortable. The music from the party is background noise.

"Why skip the party?" he asks, sounding genuinely curious.

"Same reason as you, I guess," I say, looking out at the water.

He chuckles. "Not a fan of big crowds."

"Definitely not my thing."

He shifts on the dock. "Parties make me nervous."

I get it. "They can be overwhelming."

He glances at me. "I'm glad I found you. Talking here feels easy."

I feel my cheeks heat a bit. "Yeah, it does."

He chuckles again. "We're like the 'anti-party' duo."

I laugh. "I'm good with that title."

More silence, but it's not awkward. He's watching me, and I meet his gaze. There's a warmth in his eyes that's hard to ignore.

"So, how's your day been?" Eric asks, breaking the comfortable silence.

I offer a small smile. "It's been pretty good, thanks. How about yours?"

He shrugs nonchalantly. "I've been good. How have you been lately?"

My heart flutters, but I force a smile and reply with a feigned cheerfulness, "Honestly, I've been great," even though beneath the surface, a subtle sadness lingers, hidden from his view.

He smiles, that shy yet sweet grin of his. "I'm glad to hear that."

A pause settles between us, and I find myself caught in the gravity of his gaze. It's as if he's genuinely interested in what I have to say, and that is a rare and beautiful thing.

"Honestly," I begin, my voice slightly hesitant, "it's been a bit of an emotional roller coaster for me lately."

His expression softens as he places a comforting hand on my shoulder. "I'm sorry to hear that. Anything you want to talk about?"

I take a deep breath, surprised at my own readiness to open up. "Well, my stepdad is dying—cancer—and he's been in the hospital." I pause, taking a deep breath. "It's been tough," I admit, my voice cracking slightly. "I've been trying to cope with it, but some days are harder than others."

He nods, his hand still resting reassuringly on my shoulder, his eyes never leaving mine. "If you ever need someone to talk to or just hang out with, I'm here."

I'm touched by his sincerity, his hand adding warmth to his words. It's not a forced offer of support; it's genuine kindness that reaches deep within me. I manage a weak smile. "Thank you, Eric. I appreciate that."

"My dad was in a coma for two weeks before my mom had to pull him off life support," he begins, his voice carrying a hint of vulnerability. "I was only ten, and even though I knew what was happening, it was... indescribable."

He pauses for a moment, as if reliving those painful memories. "I remember feeling so sad—like a part of me had been ripped away. I used to hide in my room, building these elaborate Lego structures, as if trying to rebuild the world around me. It was my way of coping with the loss, I guess."

I can't help but feel a deeper connection with him as he opens up about his own experience with grief.

"That sounds incredibly tough," I reply softly, my voice laced with genuine sympathy. "Losing a loved one, especially at such a young age, must have been challenging."

He nods. "Life can be really unfair sometimes. But you're not alone in this, OK?"

His words comfort me in the most unexpected way. I take a moment to compose myself before nodding. "Thank you."

"Hailey!" I turn around and see Scarlett marching toward me, her face puffy and red.

I stand up. "What's wrong?"

"This psychotic bitch poured her drink on me and

threw me in the pool," she cries, folding her arms. It's only then that I notice her shirt and pants sticking to her skin.

"Show me who did it," I demand.

She gestures toward the house, and my gaze locks onto a long-haired woman in a two-piece bathing suit, waving her middle finger in our direction. Filled with anger, I stride over in her direction.

"You think it's okay to treat people like that?" I say.

The woman smirks, her gaze assessing me from head to toe. "Who are you to butt in? This is between me and the crybaby over there."

My jaw clenches as her dismissive words hit me like a slap. "She's my best friend, and I won't stand by while you disrespect her," I assert, my voice filled with determination.

Scarlett stands by my side, her face still flushed with embarrassment and anger. "You can't just go around ruining people's nights and expect no consequences," she says, her voice shaky but defiant.

The woman's eyes narrow, and a malicious grin twists her lips. "Consequences? Oh, I'm shaking in my tiny bikini."

Fury surges within me, a torrent of emotions demanding release. "You may find this amusing, but your actions have consequences," I snap, my voice trembling with restrained anger. "You've hurt my friend, and you're going to apologize."

She crosses her arms, feigning indifference. "And if I don't?"

I take a step closer, my gaze unwavering. "Then you'll have to deal with me. And trust me, you don't want that."

Scarlett's hand tightens on my arm, a silent plea for caution. I can sense her worry and decide to leave the situation before it escalates.

Taking a deep breath, Scarlett and I turn to walk away

with Eric, who had been watching the scene unfold from a distance. But just as we begin to leave, a sudden, searing pain jolts through my scalp, and a forceful tug pulls me back into the disrespectful woman.

Fury surges within me as I whirl around to face her again, her fingers still tangled in my hair. "You just don't know when to quit, do you?" I seethe, my voice trembling with a dangerous edge.

She sneers, a twisted amusement dancing in her eyes. "Maybe I'll teach you a lesson, too." She releases her grip on my hair.

Standing up straight, I clench my fists, ready to defend myself. Strong hands grip my shoulders before the confrontation can escalate further, and I'm pulled away from the woman. It's Eric, his presence a reassuring anchor in the storm of emotions.

"Hey, she's not worth it," he says calmly, his voice steady and soothing.

I take a deep breath, trying to regain my composure as Eric's grip remains firm, a silent reminder that I'm safe.

The woman's laughter echoes behind me, mocking and infuriating. "Run along now, lovebirds."

Ignoring her taunts, I focus on Eric's calming presence, the tension slowly easing from my shoulders. Scarlett hovers nearby. Eric's voice is soft as he addresses the woman, a hint of steel underlying his words. "That's enough. It's over."

With one last glare, the woman walks away, her figure disappearing into the crowd.

"You okay?" Eric's gaze is full of concern as he meets my eyes, his fingers gentle on my shoulder.

I manage a shaky nod, gratitude flooding my chest. "Thank you, Eric."

He grins—a comforting and understanding smile that

says more than words ever could. "Let's not let her mess up the evening, okay?"

"I think I'm gonna call it a night," I say, the fatigue of the day sinking in. "Work tomorrow."

Scarlett adds, "Yeah, I'd love to head home, too."

The three of us stroll to her car, and she hands me the car keys before sliding into the passenger seat.

As I glance at Eric, I can't help but feel grateful. "Thanks for being there. It could've gone downhill fast if you hadn't stepped in."

He leans casually against the car, his expression relaxed. "That woman is one of Zack's exes."

I raise an eyebrow, understanding immediately. "Well, that explains a lot."

Just as I'm about to get into the driver's seat, Eric catches my attention by gently taking my hand. His touch is warm, his eyes sincere.

"Will you call me soon?" he asks, his tone soft.

A smile tugs at my lips. "Sure thing."

With a nod and another reassuring smile, I finally settle into the car. Eric closes the door behind me, and I start the engine. As I drive away, I can see Eric in my rearview mirror, and I can't shake the flutter in my chest.

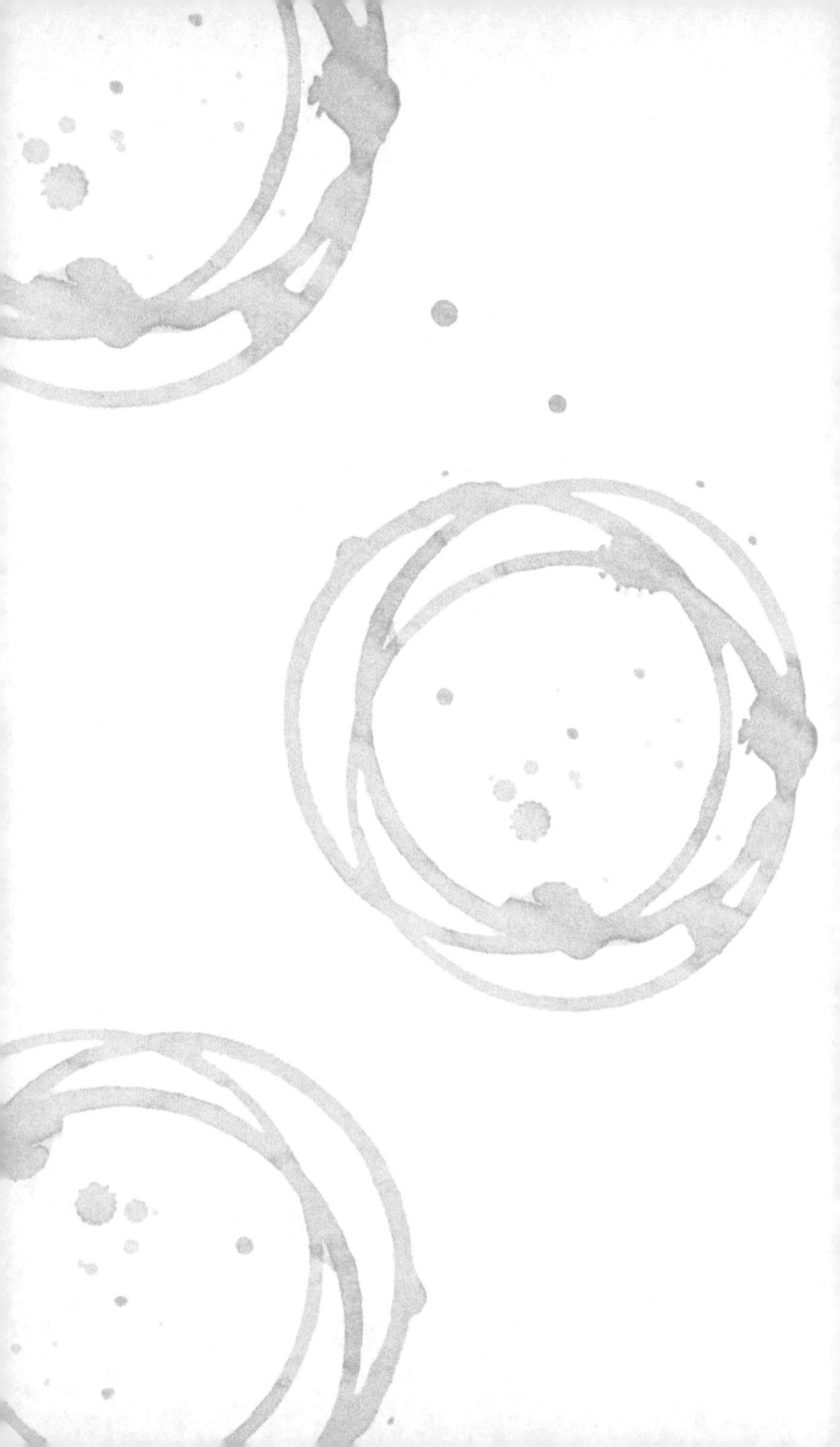

CHAPTER THIRTEEN

I sit at Scarlett's kitchen table the next morning. She's still in her bedroom, snoozing away, but for the life of me, I couldn't fall back asleep when I woke up this morning. I never fight with people, but I also won't stand to see my best friend bullied by some random bitch out of jealousy over Zack.

I scroll through my cell phone while resting my chin on the palm of my hand, and photos from last night's party on Scarlett's stories pop up. Of course, I'm not in any since I decided to leave the house only to sit on the dock. I giggle when I see a photo of her sticking her tongue out at the camera.

A notification pops up on my phone, and it's a message from my mom.

MOM

Call me right now.

My heart pounds and I quickly dial her number.
"Hey, what's up?" I ask, feeling worried.

She sounds like she's been crying when she answers, her voice all scratchy. "He's dying, baby."

I tear up. "I'm on my way," I promise before hanging up. I rush up the stairs and barge into Scar's room without knocking.

"Hey, what's going on?" she asks, surprised.

Tears stream down my face. "He's leaving me," I say, my voice breaking.

She gets up from her bed and walks over to me, giving me a tight hug to comfort me. "Put your shoes on. Let's go to the hospital."

Nodding, I walk downstairs to the living room, put on my shoes, and head out the door.

SCARLETT AND I ARRIVE AT THE HOSPITAL FIFTEEN MINUTES later. The familiar automatic doors slide open with a soft *whoosh* as we step into the antiseptic-scented air of the lobby. The clinical glow from the overhead fluorescent lights reverberates throughout the room and reflects off the linoleum floors. At the center stands the reception desk, tended to by a fatigued nurse whose eyes have borne witness to innumerable dramas that have transpired within these walls.

"Excuse me, I'm here to visit my stepdad, Ray Johnson."

She types in the computer and grabs a pen to write the room and floor number onto the visitor's passes, handing one to each of us.

"Thank you," I manage to say. Scarlett gently touches

my arm, offering silent support as we make our way to the elevators.

As the elevator doors close behind us, the tension in the air seems to grow thicker. The ascent is accompanied by a muffled ding with each passing floor, each chime echoing like a countdown to an uncertain moment. I steal a glance at Scarlett, her face a reflection of my own fear and anticipation.

The doors finally open onto the third floor, and we follow the room numbers. My heart feels like a drumbeat against my ribs as we approach the door, every step a mix of hope and trepidation.

With a deep breath, I push the door open, revealing a scene of quiet intensity that seems to hang, suspended in time.

My mom sits by the bedside, her face etched with lines of worry and sadness, her hand gently resting on the frail figure lying there. Ray appears fragile and worn against the sterile backdrop of hospital sheets and medical equipment.

His breathing is shallow, each inhale a struggle against an unseen force. The room is filled with the rhythmic beeping of machines, an electronic symphony that under-scores the gravity of the situation. Beams of sunlight filter through the curtains, casting fleeting shadows on the walls.

"Daddy," my voice cracks. He's always been my dad, despite our blood not being the same.

I step closer, my throat tightening with emotions that words cannot fully express. My mother looks up, her eyes meeting mine, and there's a mix of relief and sadness in her gaze. She stands up, giving me a hug that speaks volumes about the weight she's been carrying.

"He's been asking for you," she whispers, her voice wavering.

I nod, my eyes never leaving Ray's face.

Scarlett steps forward, her hand in mine, offering her presence as a steadfast pillar of support. We stand together, united in this moment of uncertainty, love, and shared history.

Ray's eyelids flutter open, and his tired eyes meet mine. A faint smile tugs at the corner of his lips, and it's a bittersweet sight that stirs memories of countless moments we've shared.

"Hey, champ," he rasps, his voice barely audible.

"We're here," I reply, my voice catching in my throat.

He looks at Scarlett, and there's a glimmer of recognition in his eyes. She squeezes my hand and steps forward, greeting him with a warmth that's characteristic of hers.

I try to keep my tears back, but I lose it.

Tears flow freely down my cheeks, unstoppable and cathartic. The weight of the moment, the mixture of emotions, becomes too much to bear. Scarlett wraps her arm around my shoulders, offering a comforting presence as I let go of the restraint I'd been holding onto. She's beginning to cry as well.

The world becomes a haze of colors and shadows as my vision blurs. The hospital, with its sterile walls and clinical atmosphere, fades into the background as the depth of my feelings takes center stage.

My mom joins us, her own tears mingling with mine as we share a collective release of sorrow. The barriers that I've put up to stay strong crumble in the face of this raw moment.

The room pulses with tension as Ray's breaths become ragged, each one a struggle. My mom clings to his hand, desperation in her touch. Scarlett and I stand, helpless witnesses to this fading lifeline.

An abrupt alarm blares, jolting us all. Doctors rush in,

the urgency palpable. Chaos envelops the room as medical staff work frantically around Ray's bed, words like urgent commands in a storm. Panic surges, drowning out everything else. We're shoved to the corner, where we huddle together, hearts racing in sync with the frantic beeps and commands. Machines buzz and whirl, a chaotic orchestra of life on the brink.

Then, an eerie silence falls. The doctors step away, faces frowning. My mom's sobs fill the void, a sound of anguish that chills the air.

A doctor meets my gaze, and his eyes deliver the verdict before his words do. "Time of death 7:42 AM. We're sorry."

The world narrows to that single sentence, final and irreversible. My mom collapses onto the hospital bed, resting her head on Ray's chest. Her tears are a torrent of grief. Scarlett and I remain frozen, hands clenched, hearts shattered. The room becomes a stage for sorrow, where the curtain has fallen on life's most inevitable act.

I turn around and walk out of the room. It's not that I don't want to be here, but I can't handle it.

I rush into the elevator, nurses and staff looking at me with sad eyes. My phone buzzes, but I ignore it. I know it's probably Scarlett, but I don't want to answer. I walk home, not caring how long of a walk it is.

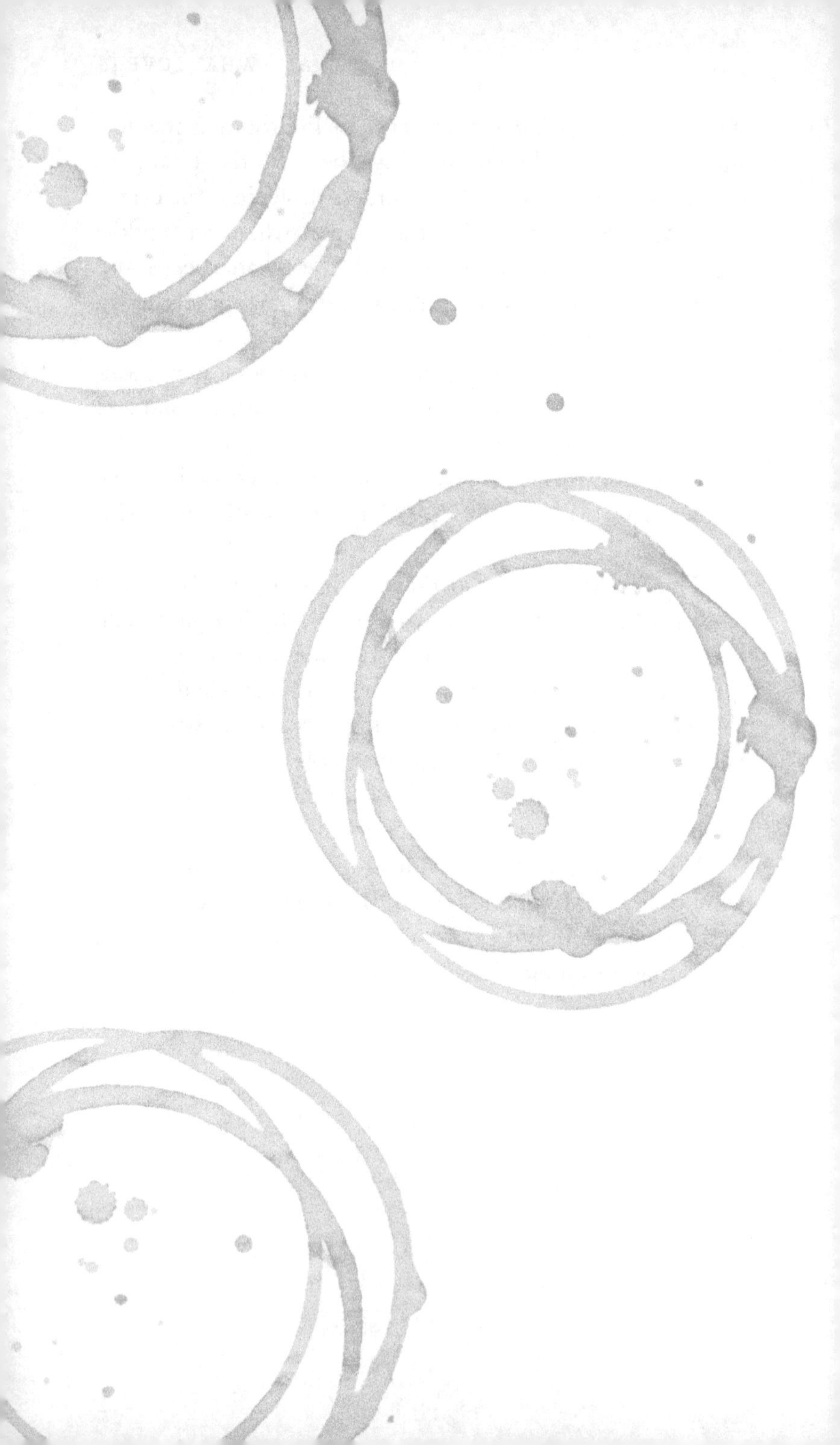

CHAPTER FOURTEEN

My room feels heavy, as if the weight of my heartbreak seeped into the walls, making it hard to breathe. It had been only an hour since I watched my step-dad's life slip away at the hospital.

An hour since I had stumbled out, tears blurring my vision as I sought refuge in the solitude of home. I needed a moment, away from the sympathetic gazes, to let the reality of it all sink in.

Lying in bed, I stare at the ceiling, unable to sleep. Thoughts of him, of the times we shared, of the laughter and warmth he brought into my life, swirl around my mind, threatening to engulf me. The quiet of the night presses in, and I know I can't bear it alone.

My fingers tremble slightly as I scroll through my contacts until I find his name: Eric. There is something about him that feels kind, genuine, comforting. Hesitating only briefly, I press the call button, waiting for him to answer. *This is probably stupid.* I go to hang up until I hear his voice on the other line. *Crap.*

"Hello?" His voice comes through, laced with surprise.

"Hey, it's Hailey," I manage, my voice wavering more than I intended. "My stepdad just passed, and I was wondering… could you come over for a little while? I don't really want to be alone right now."

There's a pause on the other end, as if he is debating his response. "Sure," he finally says, his voice cautious yet compassionate. "I'll be there soon."

"Thank you," I whisper, feeling grateful for his willingness. "I'll text you my address."

I LAY IN BED, THE SILENCE MAGNIFYING MY EMOTIONS. Fifteen minutes later, a soft knock at the door disrupts the stillness. I open it to find Eric standing there, holding a bouquet of roses.

"Hey," he says gently, his eyes searching mine. "I brought these for you."

"Thank you," I murmur, touched by his thoughtfulness. His presence alone is a balm to my wounded heart. A small smile tugs at my lips despite the sadness, and I place the flowers on the counter.

"Are you alright? Do you need me to help with anything?" he asks softly.

"Yeah, I'll be OK. I just… need some company."

He nods. "Of course, I'm here for you."

We ease onto the couch, a wordless agreement passing between us. The stillness holds a rare comfort, prompting me to open up about my stepdad. I talk about the memories we had together, the laughter and love that now mingles with emptiness. Eric sits there next to me, a bastion of unwavering support. His mere presence is a grounding force for my tumultuous emotions.

"He was something else, you know?" I manage a soft laugh, though tears well up at the corners of my eyes. "Taught me how to drive, to cook—those dad jokes that never failed."

A sympathetic smile curves his lips. "He sounds like a good man."

"He was." The simple sincerity in his words echoes the comfort I find in his company. "And now I have no dad... sort of," I admit.

He looks up at me, his expression a mix of curiosity and confusion. "What do you mean, sort of?"

I take a deep breath, choosing my words carefully. "Ray is the one who raised me. He had earned the right to walk me down the aisle and give me away, not my biological dad."

Eric's brows furrow in understanding as he pieces together the fragments of my story.

"My biological father," I begin, my voice soft and tinged with bitterness. "He hasn't ever been the dad I needed him to be. When I was a kid, he was always there but never really there, you know? He would go through these phases of being distant, happy, and then suddenly, he'd explode."

I look down at my hands, my fingers twisting in my lap. "The words he'd say... they cut deep. He would yell at me, belittle me, make me feel like I was worthless. It was like walking on eggshells all the time, never knowing what would set him off. These days, all I get are awful text messages from him," I say, feeling the weight of those hurtful words. I can't keep the bitterness out of my tone. I grab my phone, unlocking it to show him.

"You don't have to show me," he says gently, concern etched on his face.

"I want to."

He nods, understanding my need to share this part of my life. Taking the phone from my hand, he scrolls through the messages between me and my dad. The silence in the room is heavy as he reads, his expression growing darker with each passing text.

I watch his eyes trace the hurtful words, the anger, the lack of compassion. "I'm so sorry," he finally says, his voice filled with a mix of empathy and frustration.

I look at him, grateful for his understanding. "Yeah, it's difficult. But showing you… it's important. It's a part of my life, a part that's been breaking me for a long time."

Eric's gaze meets mine, his eyes holding a depth of understanding that resonates with my own pain. "Thank you for trusting me enough to share this with me."

I shrug, a small smile tugging at the corner of my lips. "It's funny, you know? I never thought I'd be sitting here, talking about all this with someone I've only known for a short while."

"I'm glad you called me," he says as he returns my phone. "I'm so sorry you have to deal with this."

I nod, a small sigh escaping my lips. "Thank you for understanding."

"How about we take our minds off this for a while? Want to watch something?"

I welcome the suggestion, a small smile returning to my lips. "That sounds nice."

Eric grabs the remote and finds a movie on a streaming service. As the movie's colorful scenes play out on the screen, its lightheartedness offers a temporary escape from the heaviness that's been lingering in the room.

As the movie progresses, I steal glances at Eric, my

heart fluttering with a mix of emotions. He seems engrossed in the movie, his features illuminated by the soft glow of the screen. Every now and then, our eyes briefly meet, creating a connection that words can't quite capture.

About halfway through the movie, I feel Eric's gaze on me, a subtle but undeniable warmth that makes my cheeks flush. I look at him and as our eyes lock, the world around us seems to fade away. The movie continues playing in the background, but our attention is solely on each other.

In our shared moment of unspoken understanding, Eric reaches out and gently places a hand on mine, his touch reassuring and comforting. Without breaking eye contact, I begin leaning, my heart racing as if it's caught in a high-speed chase.

I glance downward, but he delicately raises my chin, his touch a tender caress that quickens my heartbeat. His thumb lightly grazes my lips, sending shivers down my spine. He gazes into my eyes, as if contemplating a kiss. My gaze drifts to his lips, then returns to his, and I lean in. He wraps me in his arms, drawing me closer for a kiss. His lips are warm and soft. He gently guides me backward onto the couch. A rush of warmth courses through my body as he intensifies the kiss.

Breaking away, he leans toward my neck, planting soft kisses beneath and around my earlobe, eliciting a moan from me. His hands, both rough and gentle, slip beneath my shirt, tracing circles on my abdomen. As his hand reaches higher, I gradually sit up, pulling my shirt down.

"Eric, I can't."

He looks up at me and sits back, his eyes soft but brows narrowed with concern. "Is everything okay?"

"I'm sorry. I'm just not ready."

"Not ready for what?" he asks.

"You know… sex."

He nods, taking my hands and holding them. "It's okay, let's continue the movie."

As time passes, the movie loses its hold on us. Instead, Eric and I find comfort in each other's company. The couch, once just a piece of furniture, becomes a haven of relaxation.

His hold on me and his steady breathing both speak of understanding. Resting against him, our fingers intertwined. I feel a rare calmness, a kind of peace I haven't felt in ages.

The day's troubles and my painful history seem to fade away as I close my eyes, seeking rest in his arms. Our breaths match, creating a soothing rhythm.

In the quiet embrace of slumber, I sense healing. His touch on my back, his warmth—everything feels secure, like a shield against the world. I feel his lips press against my forehead.

As the night deepens, I surrender to sleep, nestling beside Eric on the couch.

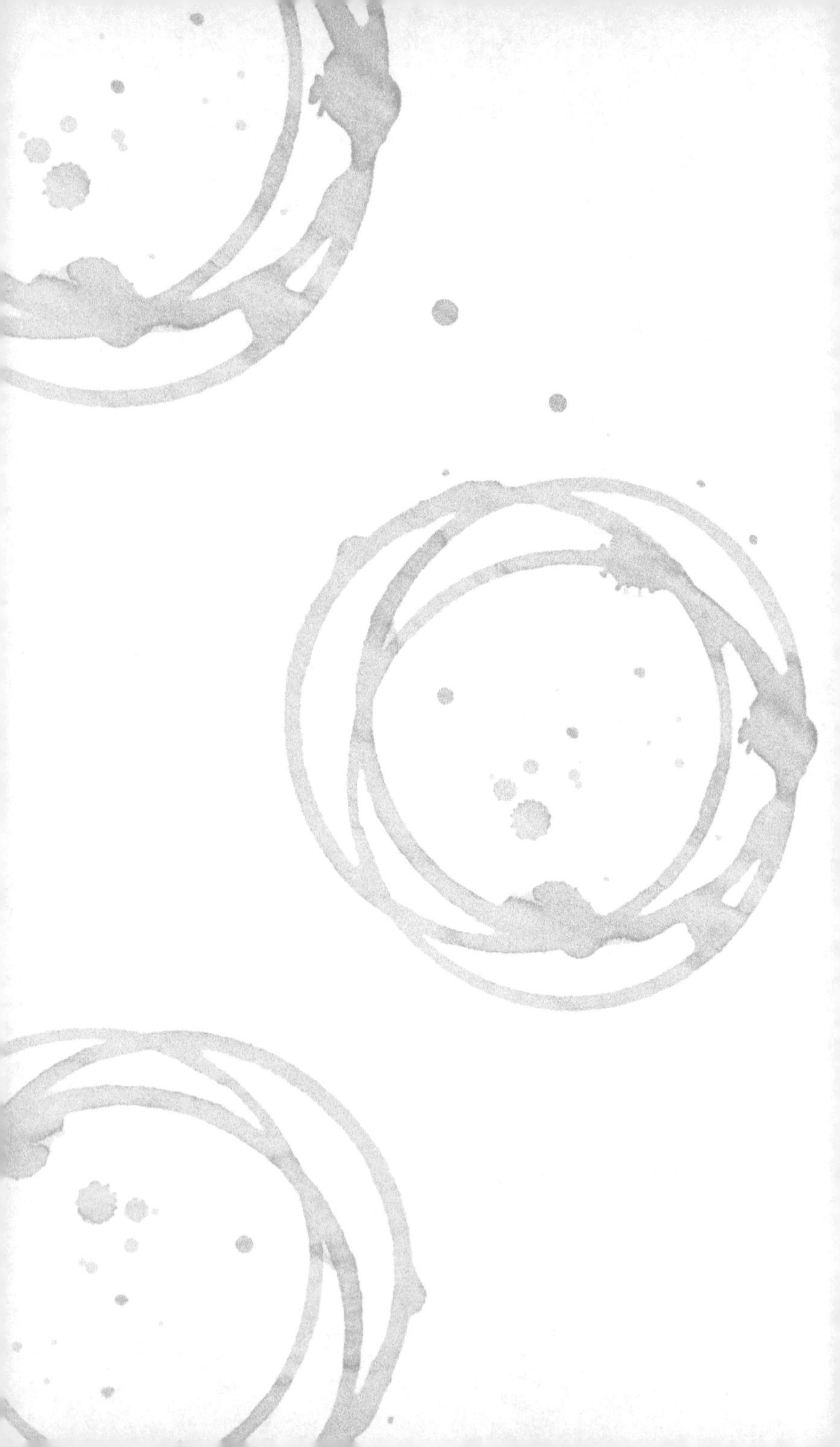

CHAPTER FIFTEEN

THE MORNING LIGHT TRICKLES INTO MY BEDROOM, painting the room in soft hues of gold. Blinking sleep from my eyes, I rub them, trying to shake off the last remnants of my dreams. As my surroundings slowly come into focus, I realize I'm in my bed, the sheets tousled around me. This isn't where I had fallen asleep last night. Did Eric carry me to my bed?

Memories of the previous evening wash over me like a wave; the laughter shared, the way his fingers brushed against mine, and that kiss on my forehead.

With a yawn, I slip my feet into my slippers and pad into the kitchen. The scent of pancakes and fresh coffee wafts through the air, a delicious wake-up call that can't be ignored. But the scent wasn't the only thing that greeted me.

Eric's standing in my kitchen with his back to me… and he's shirtless. His attention is focused solely on arranging food on a plate. I lean against the doorway, my heart fluttering as I take in the sight.

"Morning," he says, turning to me with a grin. "I hope

my breakfast is almost as good as your company."

I smile back. "You're still here?"

He chuckles, the shyness I've come to adore dances in his eyes. "Yeah, hope you don't mind. I thought maybe I could make us some breakfast. And I slept on the couch last night after carrying you to bed."

He places the plate on the island counter, and the spread is a tempting mix of pancakes and fresh fruit. Gratitude swells within me. *This man is a gentleman.* "Thank you," I say, genuinely touched. "This is amazing."

Pouring coffee into a mug, he asks, "How do you take it?"

"Two sugars, please." I watch as he carefully measures out the sugar, and when he hands me the mug, our fingers brush briefly, sending a thrill up my arm.

"Here you go," he says, his voice warm and inviting.

"Thanks." I take a sip, the taste as comforting as his presence. I find myself getting lost in his eyes, the silence between us comfortable.

"I'm really glad you came over last night. It means more to me than you know."

Eric's gaze softens, his eyes locked onto mine. "I'm glad I could be here. You can talk to me about anything. You know that, right?"

Resting against the counter, I feel a smile tugging at my lips. "Well, you've already endured my life story," I teased. "So you're stuck with me now."

His laughter is genuine and infectious. "Trust me, I'm not complaining."

A comfortable silence envelopes us again, as if the unspoken words between us are forming a bridge, connecting our hearts. I take another sip of my coffee, stealing a glance at Eric.

"So, what about you?" I ask. "I've done all the talking.

Tell me something about you that I don't know."

"Well, I was a construction worker for a few years before moving back here, and I've always wanted to learn to play the guitar. Not for any grand performances, just to strum away the day's worries in the quiet corners of my room."

"Blue collared man and an entertainer… interesting mix there." I giggle.

He looks at me with a side smile and shrugs. "Yeah, I guess."

I grab the syrup from the cabinet and pour it onto my food. "So, uh, are you still working in construction?" I ask, placing the syrup down and digging into my plate.

"Yes, I am."

"Oh, that's good," I say.

A warm smile spreads across his face. Just as the conversation settles into a comfortable rhythm, I hear my phone ping from the other room.

"Excuse me," I say and head over to my phone. I pick it up and see a text from Scarlett.

SCARLETT

Hey, are you working today?

I frown slightly, realizing that I had completely lost track of time. But I realize I want something to take my mind off Ray passing, and work can be a healthy distraction for me. Swiftly, I type out a reply as I walk back into the kitchen.

ME

Yes, I'll be there.

As I press send, I glance apologetically at Eric. "I didn't realize how late it was. I've got work," I say, stuffing my phone into my purse.

I hurry into my room, close the door, and change into a T-shirt and jeans. "Would you like a ride?" he calls out.

I smile when I walk into the living room. "That'd be nice." I slip my shoes on, and while doing so, I see him place our dishes in the sink and clean them. I grab my keys and purse.

"You ready?" I ask.

"Yes," he says while drying his hands with my kitchen hand towel. We rush out the door to his car, but before I can reach the handle, he opens the passenger side for me. I pause for a moment and give a shy smile. "Thanks," I say softly. He nods his head and I settle in while he closes the door before getting into the driver's seat.

He turns on the ignition and we head toward the café.

"Let's see what music you like." I press the power button for the radio and suddenly country music is blaring through the speakers. I laugh and look at him. "Country music?" I ask.

He looks over at me for a split second before eyeing the road again. "It's my favorite. What's yours?" he asks.

"Pop."

"Ah, figures," he chuckles.

I let out a high-pitched scoff. "What's that supposed to mean?"

"I saw a bunch of Selena Gomez albums resting on the shelf of your TV stand." He steals a glance at me.

I can't help but shake my head and chuckle. "Hey, she is amazing. Have you heard her songs?"

"I have. Catchy, but pop isn't my vibe," he says.

He pulls into the parking lot and I notice there are a few cars parked here already. He turns off the music and looks at me. "Are you sure you feel up to working today? I am sure Scarlett would give you the day off if you asked."

"Yes, I am sure. I think I need to work to keep my mind off things."

He reaches for my hand and gives a little squeeze. I squeeze back and his eyes flash down to my lips. He leans in and whispers, "Can I kiss you goodbye?"

I respond by pressing my lips to his in a soft kiss.

He pulls back slowly and asks, "When can I see you again?"

"Soon." I smirk before closing his car door and walking inside.

It's not as busy as I thought. I walk toward the register, trying to shake off the fluttering feeling in my chest from the conversation with Eric. I clock into the computer, and just as I'm about to dive into work, I feel a presence next to me.

Scarlett is leaning against the edge of the counter, a concerned look in her eyes. "Are you sure you're up for being here today? I think I'll be okay on my own if you want to take the day off."

"No, I need to be here. It'll help keep my mind focused on other things. Sorry I'm late, though. I lost track of time."

Scarlett raises an eyebrow, her eyes twinkling with curiosity. "Lost track of time, huh? Is there something you're not telling me?"

I pause and smile big. "He stayed over last night."

Scarlett lets out a gasp. "Oh really? I was wondering if you were okay after leaving the hospital. Clearly, you had yourself a distraction!"

I look down and blush.

"There's more?" she asks in a teasing tone.

"We kissed."

She smacks her leg a few times, trying not to scream excitedly with customers around.

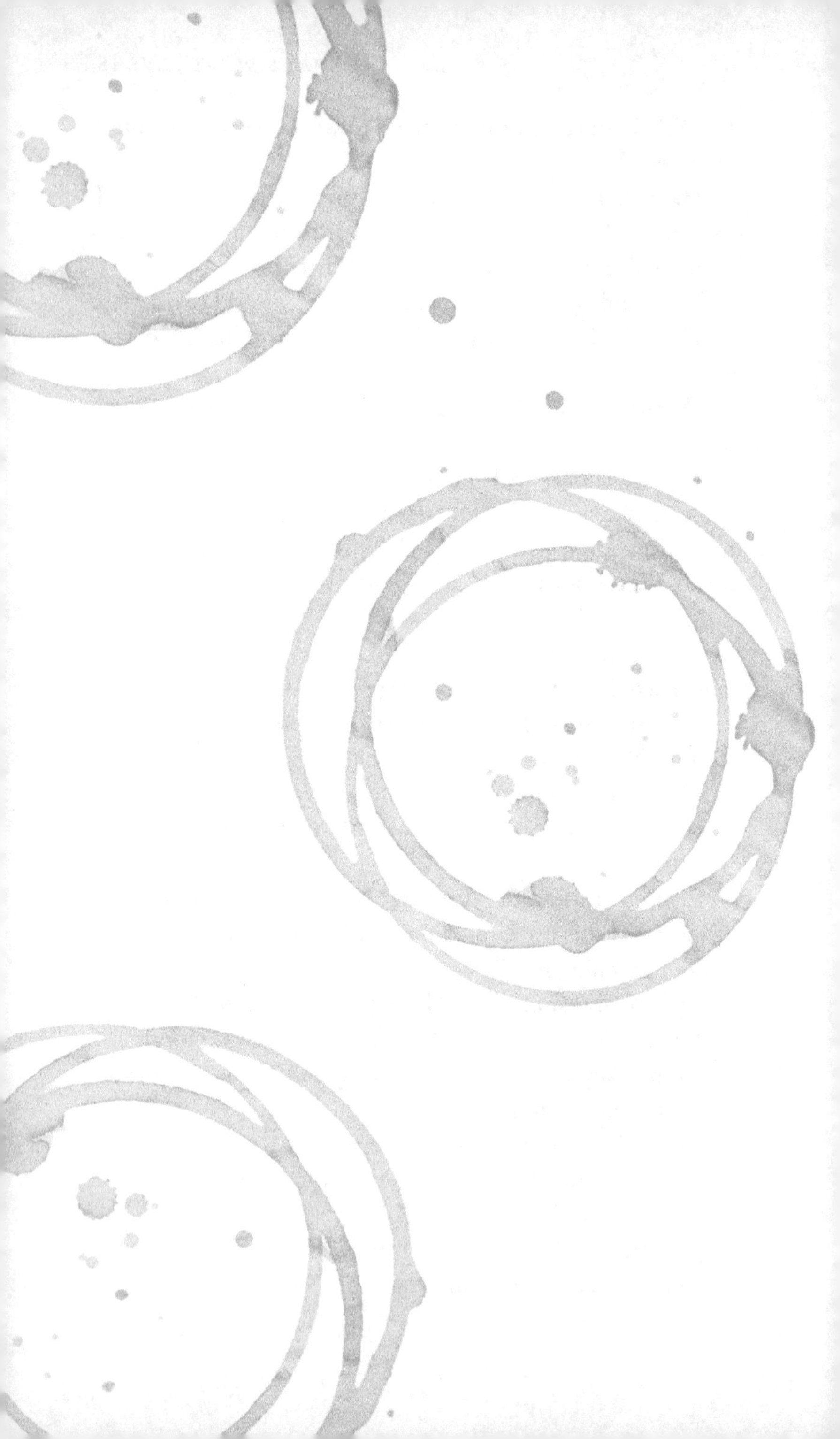

CHAPTER SIXTEEN

"Help me get these boxes of coffee filters unpacked and then we can head to your house," Scarlett says.

I nod and follow her to the back.

My mind wanders. Why is the universe punishing me? I have the shittest dad, so the world gives me a better one just to take him away? What kind of test is this? Because I feel like I'm failing miserably.

"Grab me that box cutter." She points at the top organizing rack. I reach for it and hand it to her, and she cuts open four boxes.

I begin grabbing and placing the filters underneath the cabinets, and she does the same. Back behind the kitchen is a huge pantry filled with a ton of labeled shelves.

"Do you have the permanent marker?" I ask, not being able to find it on the counter.

"Uh, yeah." She hands me the marker and I write down the count on the inventory paper.

After fifteen minutes, we are done. She turns the light off and grabs her keys from the back. We head out of the café and into her car.

I need to call my mom soon. Planning Ray's funeral is definitely stressing her out, and I need to be there for her. "Hi, I'd like to take this to go," a man says, holding a small plate of bagels.

"Sure." I grab a to-go bag and hand it to him.

"Thank you," he says.

I nod, and he walks out through the front door.

The sun lowers itself toward the horizon, casting a warm, golden glow over the charming streets of Beaufort. Each passing minute brings me closer to the moment I can finally clock out. The café has quieted down, and with a steadying breath, I pick up my phone and move away from the counter, gazing out at the familiar sights of the town I call home.

Dialing my mother's number, I feel a mix of anticipation and sadness tugging at my heartstrings. After a few rings, her voice crackles through the line, and I hold on to the phone a little tighter.

"Hailey, sweetheart." Mom's voice carries a hint of weariness and warmth. "How's your day treating you?"

Leaning against the wall, I let my gaze and thoughts start to wander, attempting to steady my voice. "Hi, Mom. It's bearable, just waiting to wrap up."

"I understand. What did you call for, honey?" she asks.

"I just wanted to check in. How are you holding up with everything?"

"I'm… trying, sweetheart. It's just really tough."

A lump forming in my throat, I blink rapidly, fending off the tears threatening to escape. "I know, Mom. Dad meant a lot to both of us." Gathering my courage, I venture further. "Do you need any help with the funeral arrangements?"

Her voice holds a glimmer of relief. "Actually, most of it is sorted. Ray and I had this planned out beforehand."

"Oh, that's good," I say.

Her tone lifted a touch. "But there's one thing. I'd like you and Scarlett to dress in dark colors, but it doesn't need to be all black. You know, for the funeral."

I nod, though she can't see me. "Of course, Mom. Where and at what time is the funeral?"

"It's at the Sunset Hill Cemetery, dear. Two o'clock on Saturday."

"Got it. Scarlett and I will be there a couple of hours early."

Her voice softens, carrying the weight of motherly love. "You're a good daughter, Hailey."

Emotion clogs my throat, and I fight to steady myself. "Thanks, Mom. Love you," I respond and end the call.

"I don't have shit to wear for the funeral," I say while digging through my drawers and closet.

"Well, let's go buy you something."

"The outfit I wear is just going to be a reminder of why I wore it. There's no point in wasting money," I explain.

"I'm just trying to be helpful," Scarlett says with a shrug.

I sigh and sit on the floor, leaning against the bed.

"Do you have anything I can wear?" I look at her with pleading eyes.

"I'm sure I do. Let's look tomorrow and see what I've got for you." She grabs my TV remote and turns it on. "Let's watch a show," she says.

I nod, stand up, and lay down on the bed as she turns an older show on, and I can't help but think about all this stress. I think about the last time my dad texted me. He only texted to tell me about his so-called blood clot. I highly doubt he has one, as he always says things like that to make me feel bad for him for no real reason. He has manipulated my mom and me that way for years.

There are moments where I want to believe him because what if he is sick and I ignore it because of the lies or the way he treats me? But then I remember all the lies he has told me, and I find myself not caring if he is telling the truth.

I close my eyes and drift off to sleep.

CHAPTER SEVENTEEN

I SMILE AS I READ THE TEXT FROM ERIC AND THEN MY phone is snatched from my hands like a fish on a hook.

"Damn it, Scarlett, give it back!" I demand. Scarlett reads the message out loud.

"Oh, honey, he is IN LOVE with you!" she laughs.

"I just met him, not possible!"

"It can be!" She hands me my phone back.

"No way."

"Look, I'm just glad you're giving this guy a shot. He seems really nice."

"Yeah, he does, doesn't he?" I blush.

She squeals and stands up. "Alright, let's head out for breakfast and then go find you some clothes, mkay?"

"Okay, but no talking about boys."

She grabs her purse and slips her shoes on. "That's no fun."

We arrive at our favorite food place, Oceanview Dinner, which sits right on the beach. It's always busy and full of people no matter what time of day it is. As we walk in, I'm hit with the smell of eggs and bacon. The booths are dark brown leather, with wooden tables, and many people are seated already.

"Hi, just a party of two?" the waitress asks.

"Yes," Scarlett says.

"Okay, follow me." The waitress stops in front of a booth near the window with a clear view of the ocean and gestures for us to sit.

"What can I get you started with?" she asks.

"We'll each take a Pepsi," I say.

"Coming right up." The waitress goes to the back, and we look at each other and laugh.

"I'm happy that we both like the same thing. It means I don't have to order for myself most of the time," Scarlett says.

"I'm your voice, it's all good," I joke.

We both grab the menu and look it over. Even though we know what we are ordering, we look anyway in case we decide to be spontaneous.

"Hailey?" a familiar, deep voice calls for me. I look up and see Eric standing near Scarlett, smiling at me. Scar looks up at him, then at me, winking.

"What are you doing here?" I ask. This man makes me blush more than anyone ever has.

"Oh, I'm just seeing more of the city. Figured I'd stop by and grab some food while doing so."

"Would you like to sit with us?" Scar asks.

I widen my eyes.

"Oh, sure! Thanks," he says.

I scoot over and he sits next to me. His cologne smells refreshing, and my heart races.

"I heard you stayed over at Hailey's the other night."

I kick her in the shin underneath the table and she gives me a *chill out face.*

"Oh, uh, yeah, she called and said she needed company."

"I also know you two kissed."

My face turns bright red. I can really feel it. I purse my lips and cover my eyes.

"Scarlett, shut up," I laugh.

Eric looks at me and places his arm over the top of the booth with a big smile. I sense he is loving this.

"It was a good kiss," he says.

Oh my god, the butterflies are worse now.

"Anyway, today is going to be interesting," Scarlett says.

"Yeah," I reply.

"Why's that?" Eric asks me.

"Oh, uh, picking out clothes for the funeral on Saturday."

Eric's smile fades, and his expression softens. "If there's anything I can do to help or support you, please let me know."

"Thanks," I say, touched by his sincerity. "It's been a tough few days, but I'm lucky to have Scarlett here with me."

He nods, understanding. "Having good friends around makes a world of difference." He pauses, then continues, "So, Hailey, could I talk to you about something?"

I side eye Scarlett and she nods.

"Sure," I reply. Eric stands up and offers me his hand. I accept, and he gently grasps my hand and helps me from the booth. He doesn't let go while leading me outside on the back patio.

He stands in front of me, his face serious, but a small smile appears.

"I know this is bad timing, but I can't stop thinking about you." He looks me in the eyes ever so sweetly, like he's wanting to say more but doesn't want to move too fast.

As his words sink in, I can feel my heart rate increasing. Despite the bustling sounds of the city and crashing waves around us, it is as if time stands still, leaving only the two of us in this moment. I can't help but feel a mixture of surprise and delight at his confession.

"I... I wasn't prepared for that," I confess, feeling embarrassed. "And yeah, the timing is complicated."

He lets out a nervous chuckle, his fingers tightening slightly around mine. "Yeah, I know. I promise I'm not trying to make things more difficult for you. It's just that spending time with you the other night, that kiss, it felt... right."

I'm caught between his earnest gaze and the whirlwind of thoughts in my mind. I feel a rush of emotions—excitement, caution, curiosity—all intermingling within me.

"I feel the same way." As I look into his eyes, I can't help but notice how blue they are. The sun shining in them creates a slight sage green color. "Would you mind going to the funeral with me?" I ask.

He sighs, but not in an uncomfortable or hesitant way—he sounds relieved. "If you would like me to be there, yes, I will go with you."

I smile. "I have to head back inside. I'll text you the details soon, okay?"

"Okay." He pulls me into a gentle hug, arms wrapped around my waist, and I hug him back before pulling away.

"Bye," I say, tucking my hair back behind my ear and heading toward the doors.

"Bye, Hailey." He waves.

I join Scarlett back at our table.

"This omelet looks amazing." I pick up the fork and take a bite.

"What did he want?" she asks.

I grab my Pepsi and take a sip from the straw. "You were right."

"About what?"

"He likes me."

"No," she says sarcastically, before taking a drink.

"I'm scared, you know."

"No one is going to break your heart on my watch, and if they do, they'll go six feet underground."

I chuckle and continue eating.

I'm glad she's my best friend.

"I feel sick," I say, while holding my head.

"Maybe you shouldn't eat so fast," Scarlett says, while unlocking her front door. We left the restaurant less than twenty minutes ago and my stomach is churning and my head is pounding.

"Doesn't make sense, I eat that omelet weekly."

"Maybe it's the nerves getting to you," she says while opening the door. We walk in the house and I slowly make my way up the stairs.

I shrug. "Maybe."

I lie down on her bed while she rummages through her closet.

"Are you wanting a dress or pants?"

"Dress is fine," I say.

"How about this?" She pulls out a purple, skin-tight v-neck dress.

I sit up slightly and look. "That's fine. Do you have flats to go with it?"

"Sure do!" She picks up a black pair of flats from the back corner of the closet and places them on her desk.

"Great, you know I can't do heels."

"Oh no, we can't have another prom night." She laughs.

"Hey, you should've made sure I didn't drink that night."

"Girl, you needed to loosen up. I stayed sober, so you didn't have to." She places her dress on the hook hanging on the back of the door and sits beside me.

"What time are we meeting with your mom?"

"Noon, Saturday," I say.

She whips out her phone and starts typing away, then places it down on the desk to charge.

"What'd you just do?" I raise a brow.

"Made sure the town knew the café was closed."

"Can you go grab me some medicine for my head?" I ask.

"Yeah, want a snack?"

"Got any applesauce?"

"For you, it's always stacked in the fridge!"

I give a small laugh. "Thanks."

She walks out of the room. "Be right back!" she says, closing the door slightly behind her.

"Hailey, wake up," Scarlett whispers as she shakes my shoulder.

"Shit, when did I fall asleep?" My voice is raspy and groggy.

"You dozed off before I came back upstairs with your snack and medicine."

"What time is it?" I ask.

"Seven in the evening." She turns the lamp on. "Here, take your medicine," she says. I reach for the glass of water in her hand, swallow the water, and give it back.

"I feel like I've been hit by a truck."

"You look like it." She looks at me with soft eyes.

"I'm gonna take a hot bath," I say.

She nods and I slowly pick myself up from the bed and grab my phone, taking it with me to her bathroom.

I turn the tub on and pour the muscle-relaxing bubbles in the water and undress, placing my clothes in her hamper.

I step into the tub and sit, allowing the water to flow on my feet while I lie back. Something about the noise of the water filling the tub while I'm in it makes me more relaxed.

Grabbing my phone from the shelf next to the tub, I tap Eric's name and text him.

ME

> Meet me at Sunset Hill Cemetery at noon on Saturday.

Dots appear on the screen and he replies.

ERIC

> See you then, sweetheart.

Locking my phone and grasping it tightly, I press the top of it against my quivering chin. Tears are welling up, threatening to overflow, and I carefully place my phone down, fearing I might let it slip from my trembling grip. The tears break free, tracing a path down my face, mingling with the running stream.

My body convulses with sobs. My arm instinctively wraps around my stomach, as if trying to hold myself together, while my hand clings desperately to my quivering lips, trying to contain the anguish that's threatening to erupt in a guttural cry.

The door opens and Scar rushes in, kneeling down and turning the water off. Not caring that she's fully dressed when she gets in with me, she sits down and grabs my head with one hand, pulling me into a hug with her free arm and resting her chin on my head.

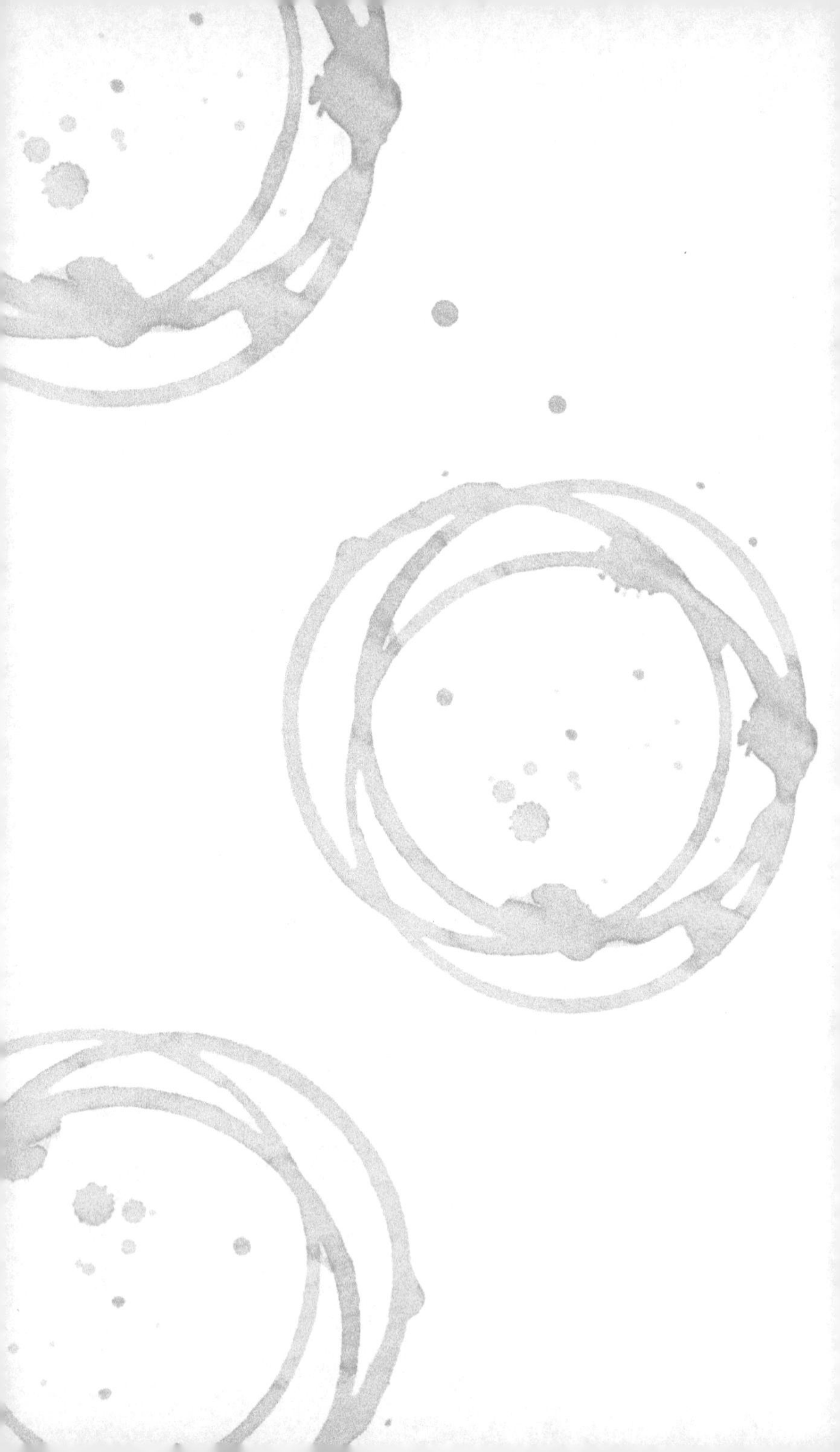

CHAPTER EIGHTEEN

S̲ATURDAY ROLLS AROUND FASTER THAN I HOPED. I ROLL out of bed and head to the bathroom to brush my teeth. Looking into the mirror, I notice my eyes are baggier than ever. I grab the face wash and begin to wash, rinse, and apply my moisturizer. I pull out the concealer and begin dabbing some with my ring finger on the dark circles appearing.

"You okay?" Scarlett asks, while leaning against the bathroom door.

I look at her through the mirror and nod. "No, not really."

Putting the concealer back, I grab my mascara and go over my lashes as quickly and gently as possible, careful not to make a mess on my eyelids.

"Sorry about the past week. Thank you for being there," I say while zipping the makeup bag up and turning to face her.

"Don't be. You're dealing with a lot. I'm here, always." She squeezes my shoulder. "I'm going to take a shower in the downstairs bathroom. Take the time you need to get ready."

Can today be over already?

I slip into my dress and shoes and grab a black scrunchie, tying my hair up in a high ponytail. My cell says eleven, which means it's time to leave to meet my mom.

It's been an hour since Scarlett said she was going to shower. "Scar, are you ready?" I holler.

"Yes, do you have your charger? I can't find mine."

I look around and unplug the USB cord from the charging brick on the wall, carrying it with me down the stairs. "Here," I say, handing it to her.

"Thanks."

"Let's go," she says, and we walk out of the house and settle into the car.

Thirty minutes later, we arrive at the cemetery. Scarlett parks next to my mom's silver sedan in the gravel lot. With a shaky breath, I say, "I just want to sit here for a bit before I get out."

"Okay, I'll stay right here with you."

"No, don't worry, go meet Mom, please."

"You sure?" she asks with a concerned tone.

"Yes, just tell her I'm taking a moment."

"Okay." She unbuckles her seatbelt and opens the car

door. "See you in there."

Some family members are already here. Family friends of his that I'm also close with are beginning to arrive. I look at the road and notice a dark gray pickup truck pulling in. It's Eric. He's ten minutes early. I smile and grab my purse from the floor and step out of the car while he steps out of his truck.

"Hi," I say, walking up to him.

"Hi." He looks up at me with a smile. "You look beautiful."

He's wearing a black button-up, long sleeve shirt with a black tie, dress pants, and shoes. "You look great, too," I compliment him.

He reaches his hand out. I accept, and we intertwine our fingers. "Thank you for coming."

"Like I said, I'm here for you. What is your mom's name?" he asks.

"Carly," I say.

We walk over to the huge tent where my mom and Scarlett stand talking to people around us.

"Oh, honey," my mom says. I gently pull my hand away from Eric's and give my mom a hug. Her dark purple dress matches her dark purple heels, and her long brunette hair rests over one shoulder.

"Who's this?" she asks, looking at Eric.

Before I can introduce him, he beats me to it.

"Hi, I'm Eric. Hailey's friend." He extends his arm out, offering to shake her hand, and she accepts.

"Hi, call me Carly. Hailey, you didn't tell me you were

dating someone."

"Oh, we're just getting to know one another."

"Mhm, I see." She smiles knowingly.

"I'm going to find a seat. Scar, want to come with us?" I ask.

"Yes."

We find a spot close to the closed casket. I sit just a few steps from the open grave. My fingers trace the edges of my dress, a nervous habit that surfaces whenever emotions overwhelm me. The world seems muted.

Sinking into the chair, memories of Ray flood my mind. His laughter, his guidance, his unwavering support —they all rush back, making my chest tighten with gratitude and sorrow. The soft whispers of leaves and distant voices of the attendees merge with the officiant's somber words.

The casket is adorned with flowers and the weight of finality. The eulogies paint a vivid picture of a man who touched many lives, but my mind lingers on our personal moments—the way he taught me to drive a car, his patient reassurance after heartbreaks, his presence that filled rooms with warmth.

I clench my hands in my lap, my eyes fixed on the ground. A rush of emotions floods me—the pain of loss, the depth of gratitude, the ache of an uncertain future. I swallow hard, focusing on the chair beneath me, as if it could keep me steady.

Eric grabs my hand, squeezing it gently and leaning toward my ear. "Deep breaths, sweetheart."

As I stand and approach the casket, a breeze dances through the air. I close my eyes briefly, letting the wind brush against my cheeks like a gentle caress. My heart remains heavy, but there's comfort in knowing that others share in this grief and that I'm not alone in my sadness.

Scarlett offers a small smile, her hand resting on my arm.

"Thank you for being here with Hailey," Scarlett says to Eric.

"It's the least I could do," he replies.

"I miss you so much, Dad," I murmur, my fingers tracing the engraving on the casket. Tears trickle down my cheeks, the ache in my chest almost unbearable.

The rest of the day passes in a blur—hugs, shared memories, the company of friends and family. As the sun sets, casting a warm golden hue over the cemetery, I find myself sitting beside Ray's final resting place, the silence a space for reflection.

"I don't know how to do life without you," I admit to Ray, though it's more to myself than anything.

"You don't have to do it alone," Eric says softly, breaking me out of my thoughts. "You have people who care about you, who want to help carry the weight."

He sits next to me and pulls me into a hug. I lean into his touch, finding comfort in his words.

"Could you take me home?" I plead.

"Sure." He stands up and takes my hand and we walk toward Scarlett.

"Hey, I'm going to have Eric take me home."

"Okay, call me when you get there." She gives me a hug.

We sit in the driveway of my house. I haven't made a move to get out yet, wanting to sit in the silence a moment longer. I finally feel ready and make a move to open the door. Eric stops me and steps out of the truck, a small smile playing on his lips as he walks around to my side of the truck. The sun shines a bright glow down on us. He opens the passenger door, a gesture so simple yet incredibly endearing.

As I step out, the night air wraps around me, and he closes the door with a soft thud. My heart quickens as he walks beside me, his stride matching mine. The path to my front door seems longer tonight, as if time had decided to slow down for us. With each step, my gratitude wells up, and I find the courage to voice it.

"Thank you for being there. It meant a lot to me," I say, the sincerity of my words echoing in the hushed night.

"I'm glad I could be there for you," he says, his hands finding refuge in his pockets.

And then, the question hung in the air, an unspoken invitation to something more. "Can I, uh, take you out for dinner soon?" he asks, his vulnerability adding a touch of charm.

A smile dances at the corner of my lips. "How about Tuesday night?" I respond, my voice carrying a blend of hope and excitement.

The words, "Sounds like a date" leave his lips, his proximity sending a delightful shiver down my spine. His lips, soft and warm, brush against my cheek, imprinting a memory that lingers like a sweet melody.

"Have a good night, Hailey," he whispers, his breath brushing against my skin like a promise.

"You too," I reply, my voice carrying a sincerity that surpasses mere politeness. As I watch him walk away, his figure illuminated by the soft glow of the streetlights, I feel conflicted.

Each detail, each word, is etched into my heart.

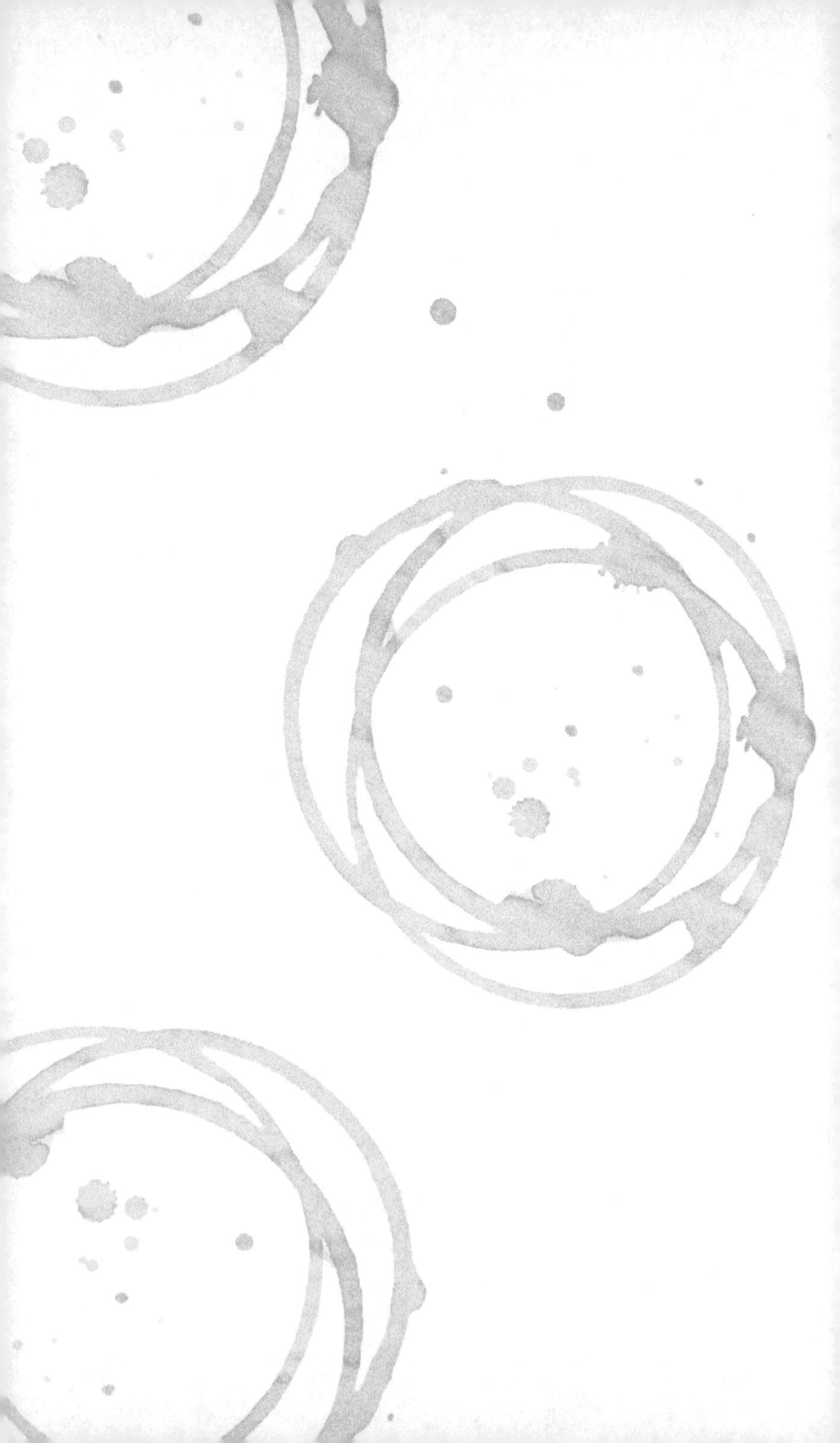

CHAPTER NINETEEN

THE NEXT FEW DAYS WHISKED BY, LEAVING ME IN A HAZE OF emotions that swung between nervousness and excitement. Tuesday evening arrives, and as the sun dips below the horizon, I stand in front of my mirror, my reflection revealing anticipation and doubt.

My fingers hesitate over my clothes, unsure of what would be right for the occasion. After a series of changes, I settle on a simple, but elegant dress. I carefully slip into it and look in the mirror. The dress accentuates my curves, but my reflection also shows the slight crease of my brow, the self-conscious tuck of a strand of hair behind my ear. Uncertainty tugs at the edges of my thoughts.

Is this too much? Too little? Does it make me look awkward? My heart flutters in response to the questions in my mind. The dress draws attention to my features, but the mirror also shows the slight crease of my brow, the self-conscious tuck of a strand of hair behind my ear. It's more than just a dress; it's a piece of the puzzle that I hope fits seamlessly into this unfolding connection.

As I gaze at myself in the mirror, I try to summon a

smile, to reassure myself that this is a step worth taking. The memory of his lips grazing my cheek warms my heart, and in that warmth, a hint of happiness emerges. I can't help but wonder if Eric saw the unease that hid behind my smile.

As I stand lost in my thoughts, the doorbell chimes, startling me. My heart leaps in my chest, excitement and nerves flooding over me. Taking a deep breath, I smooth my dress and make my way to the door. With each step, the sound of my own heartbeat seems to grow louder, an erratic rhythm that mirrors my emotions.

I swing the door open to see Eric looking as charming as ever. His gaze meets mine, eyes wide as he looks me up and down. His eyes hold a warmth that eases some of my apprehension. With a small smile playing on his lips, he holds out a bouquet of roses, their vibrant colors of blue and purple contrasting beautifully with the evening's fading light.

"You look beautiful," he breathes. "These are for you."

I take the bouquet, my heart racing. "Thank you."

The corners of his lips curl into a smile that reaches his eyes.

"Come on in," I offer.

As he enters the room, I glide over to the sink. Carefully, I cradle the bouquet in my hands, lowering them into the vase. The clear, cool water rises around the stems, enveloping them in a refreshing embrace. With deliberate grace, I set the vase down on the table, allowing the vibrant blooms to steal the spotlight. I look at Eric. "So, where are we going tonight?" I ask, curiosity bubbling in my voice.

He shuffles his feet, a hint of shyness in his smile. "Well, that's the thing, Hailey. It's a surprise," he replies with a wink, his tone gently teasing. "I've got something special planned for us."

My curiosity ignites, an ember of excitement growing within me. His playful secrecy intrigues me. "Oh, come on, give me a hint," I prod, unable to contain my eagerness.

Eric's eyes sparkle as he considers my request. "Alright, I'll give you this much: it involves sand and a basket."

His words weave an intriguing picture. I can't help but chuckle. "You know how to pique my curiosity, don't you?"

He shrugs. "Just doing my best to make it a memorable night." Eric takes a step closer, his smile softening. "Are you ready to go?"

My heart skips a beat. With a nod and a smile, I reply, "Absolutely."

He walks to the front door, opening it and extending his arm out. "Ladies first."

I smile and walk through, and he follows. "So, how far is this surprise of yours?" I ask while he opens the passenger door for me.

Eric's lips curl into a playful smile. "Not too far," he replies, his tone a mix of mystery and intrigue. "But you'll see soon enough."

As Eric pulls into the parking lot of the beach, the moon hangs low in the ink-black sky, casting a silver glow upon the waves that lap gently at the shore. "We're here," he announces, his voice tinged with playfulness.

My eyes are wide with wonder. "The beach is always fun!"

"Yep, but there's something special waiting. Trust me." He holds out his hand, and I take it.

With my heart racing, I step out of the truck and onto

the sandy path that leads toward the shore. I slip my shoes off and hold them.

A trail of soft, twinkling lights guides my gaze to an area adorned with blankets and cushions. A small table stands elegantly, fake candles flickering in the ocean breeze.

I can't help but cover my mouth in astonishment. "Eric, is this…?"

He nods, his eyes holding a warmth that melts into my very soul. "A surprise picnic on the beach. Our first real date."

"Did Scarlett put you up to this?" I ask.

"I may have asked her what your ideal first date was," he says.

Tears gather in my eyes. "I can't believe you've done all of this."

Eric chuckles, his thumb brushing away a stray tear from my cheek. "You deserve it. I wanted tonight to be about us," Eric says as we both take a seat at the table.

The soft glow of the candles creates an intimate cocoon around us. I take in the spread of food before us, my stomach rumbling in response to the delectable array. "Wow, this looks incredible. Did you make all of this?" I ask.

Eric chuckles, leaning back on his cushion. "I wish I had the culinary skills to take credit, but no. Made from the local deli." He grins, his eyes sparkling. "I thought we could indulge a little tonight. Here, try this," he says, handing me a slice of juicy watermelon.

I take a bite. "Nothing better than fresh watermelon. I love fruit."

"I figured. When making pancakes the other day, I noticed a bunch of grapes and cantaloupe and a near empty plastic bowl of watermelon in your fridge."

"So, tell me something about you that I don't know," I ask, quirking an eyebrow.

He feigns a thoughtful expression. "Well, I used to be a professional yo-yo enthusiast."

I burst out laughing, unable to contain myself. "No way!"

He nods, his expression deadpan. "Yep, I traveled the world competing in yo-yo tournaments."

I wipe away a tear of laughter. "I'm sorry, I just can't picture it."

He grins, the corners of his eyes crinkling. "Alright, alright, I may have exaggerated that one a bit. But I did go through a phase where I thought I was the yo-yo champion of my neighborhood."

I laugh, feeling a sense of comfort settle between us. "Well, that's definitely a unique hobby."

"Tell me something unexpected about yourself," Eric asks, his gaze curious.

I ponder for a moment, thinking of a tidbit that might catch him off guard. "Well, not many people know that I used to be an avid book collector."

He raises an eyebrow. "Books?"

I nod, feeling a smile of fondness form on my lips. "Yes, I used to have shelves filled with books of all kinds. I loved exploring different worlds within the pages."

Eric's eyes brighten. "That's fascinating. Do you still read a lot?"

"I do, but my collection isn't as extensive as it used to be. Life happened, and I had to make some space."

"Darn, that sucks. My mom used to read a lot."

"What kind of books?" I ask.

"Mostly romance."

I nod. "My mom likes those, too. Ohh, is that Cheez

Whiz? I love Cheez Whiz!" I reach for the small container of crackers and metal canister.

"Sometimes it's the simple things that bring the most joy."

"Indeed."

As I look at Eric, I realize what I like so much about him. Not only can I be myself around him, but it feels like we've known each other forever. The silence isn't awkward and I don't feel the need to break it. "You know, this might be the fanciest Cheez Whiz experience I've ever had."

"Well, I aim to impress," he jokes.

Our laughter dances on the night breeze, mingling with the soft glow of the candles. "You're definitely succeeding," I say.

A sudden chill runs down my spine, and I shiver involuntarily.

"You okay?" Eric asks, his voice filled with concern.

I smile, appreciating his attentiveness. "Just got a little chill from the breeze."

He glances around and then back at me. "Hold on a second."

He grabs a blanket, unfolding it and gently draping it over my shoulders. His cologne envelops the air around me, and the gentleness of his gesture stirs a different kind of sensation within me.

"Thank you," I breathe, the blanket instantly chasing away the chill.

His gaze meets mine. With a tender smile, he leans in, and my heart quickens in response. As our lips meet in a gentle, lingering kiss, a rush of warmth courses through me. As his lips meet mine, I can't help but respond, my heart racing in my chest.

When we finally pull away, our breaths mingling with the sea breeze, our eyes lock onto each other's. There's a sense of wonder in the air, as if we've uncovered something precious in the midst of the night's magic.

"Hailey," Eric whispers.

I meet his gaze, my heart pounding. "Yes?"

His fingers brush against mine, and he takes a deep breath before speaking. "Would you like to stay at my place tonight?"

I return his gaze, and a smile tugs at the corners of my lips, my heart guiding me forward. "I'd really like that."

Breaking the spell, Eric stands up, a determined yet gentle expression on his face.

"Let's head out," he says.

He stands up and takes my hand, helping me up, and we gather the picnic items, folding the blankets and carefully packing them away. Then I toss the trash into the nearest can.

It takes a couple trips to put all the items in the truck.

Once everything is neatly packed, he turns toward me, extending his hand with an inviting gesture. I grab the blankets from him and, without hesitation, I slip my hand into his, our fingers intertwining naturally.

The connection feels right, as if our hands were meant to fit together. As we begin to walk back toward the truck, the path is illuminated by the soft glow of the moonlight. The waves continue their gentle serenade, harmonizing with the rhythm of our steps.

As I sit on his couch, I look around his living room. He has soft music playing on his smart TV and fake candles lit on little shelves on the walls and on his coffee table. His small cabin house is cozy.

"Tonight has been incredible so far. Thank you," I say, sipping a glass of wine he poured for me.

"I had fun, too," he says while lighting his fireplace.

"This place is beautiful," I whisper.

"I'm glad you like it," he says with a warm smile, his gaze meeting mine. The soft crackling of the fireplace fills the room, casting a gentle, flickering light across the cabin's rustic interior.

My phone buzzes, and I pull it out of my purse. *"Dad"* texted me after not hearing from him for a couple of weeks.

DAD

I'm sorry about Ray. Love you.

I roll my eyes and lock my phone.
"Everything okay?" Eric asks, sitting down next to me.
Before I can put it back in my purse, it buzzes again.
I nod and open the message.

DAD

Why do you keep fucking ignoring me?

Ignoring my dad's texts, I throw my phone down in my purse and gently grab Eric's face, turning it toward me. I lean in to kiss him and he meets me halfway. The kiss starts slow, but soon Eric pulls me onto his lap as the kiss deepens. With his hands on my hips, we explore each other's mouths, my mind pushing aside all thoughts of my father and focusing on the man in front of me.

The moment seems to hang in the air, suspended in desire. The soft glow of the room's candles plays upon our intertwined figures, casting fleeting shadows across the walls. As our lips meet again, a surge of electricity courses through me, every touch igniting a fire that had long been smoldering. His hands on my hips feel both reassuring and possessive, pulling me closer to him as if we are two halves finally reuniting. He glides his fingers across my arm, tracing gentle patterns on my skin and sending shivers down my spine.

Without breaking the kiss, his hands reach my thigh, sliding beneath my dress, and I let out a quiet moan. My heart pounds against my chest as he begins to move his hand higher.

He lifts me up from the couch and takes me into his bedroom, lying me down on his bed. I sit up and pull off my dress before moving to unbutton his shirt. He trails kisses up my neck. "You're so beautiful," he whispers in my ear. I giggle slightly when he slips my lacy panties down my legs, tossing them to the side.

"Are you sure?" he asks me.

I look at him with soft eyes. "I'm sure."

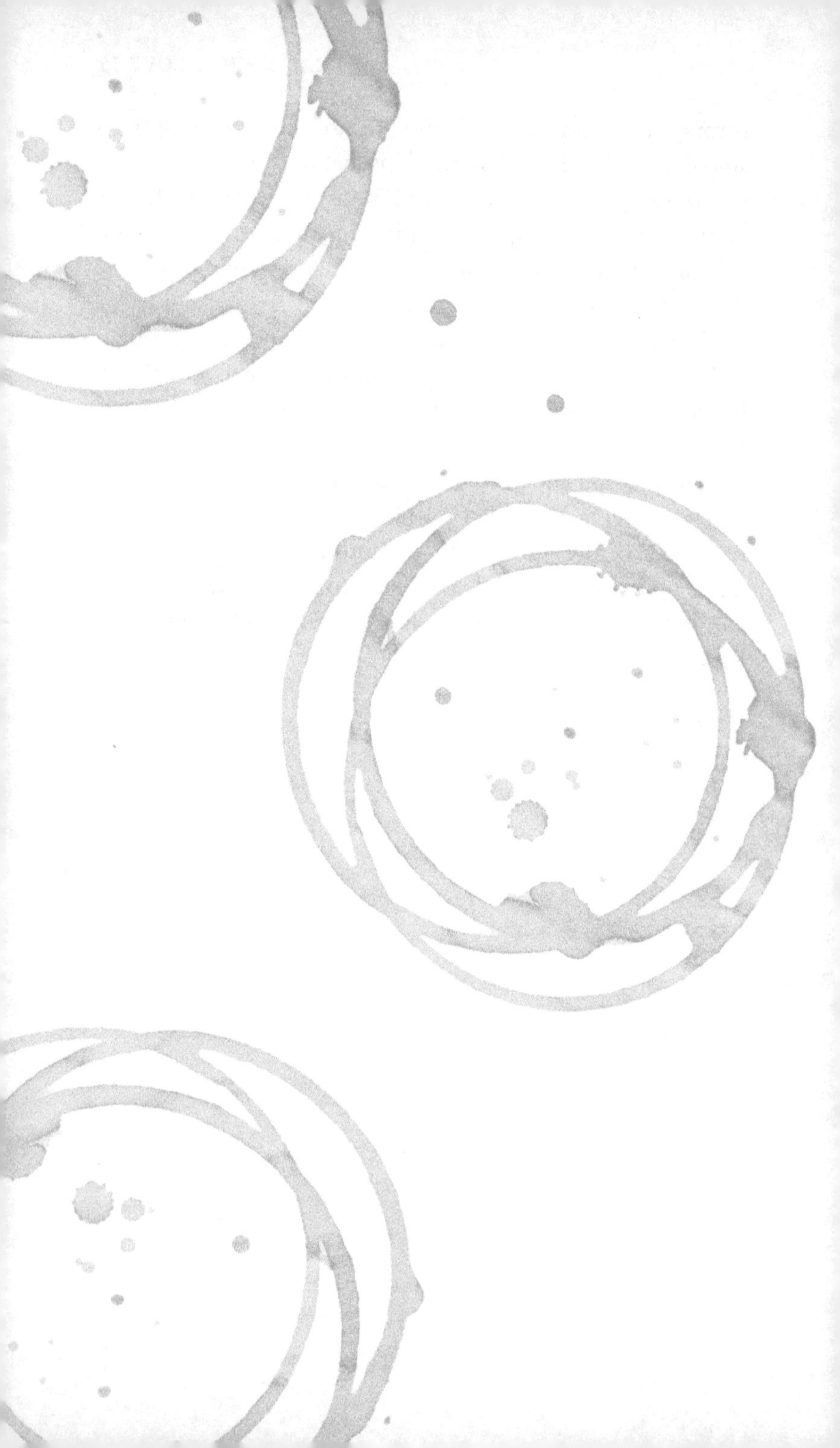

CHAPTER TWENTY

The alarm on my phone wakes me up. I quickly tap the snooze button, rub my eyes, and smile when I realize what had happened last night. I turn to look at Eric's side of the bed but frown when I don't see him. Standing up from the bed, I slip on my underwear and dress. I notice a small sticky note on his pillow.

Good morning, beautiful. I had to leave for work. There is coffee and a blueberry muffin on the counter. See you later, I hope?—Eric.

A smile creeps on my face at the sweet note and thoughtfulness of breakfast. But the moment fades when I realize I don't have my car. I grab my phone, dialing Scarlett.

"Hey! What's up?" she asks.

"Hey, do you mind picking me up from Eric's?"

"Sure. Why don't you have your car?" she asks.

"He took me out last night and we sort of… crashed here."

"I'm sure there was more than crashing," she jokes.

"Shush," I reply.

"Oh, so there is more?" She squeals with excitement. "Pin me your location, you owe me details!" She hangs up. I look at my phone, rolling my eyes while sending her my location.

WHILE I WAIT FOR SCARLETT, I TAKE THE TIME TO EXPLORE the cabin. It's clean, no garbage anywhere, definitely not messy like my ex-boyfriends' homes. As I head into the hallway, I notice pictures of him and some other people. "2010… Dad and me," I read. Oh wow, he's the spitting image of his dad. I frown, remembering him mentioning he passed away. Photos of Eric and his mom hang on the wall, bringing a smile to my face. He seems really close to her.

A loud honk interrupts my thoughts, and I rush to the window, peeking through the curtains. Scarlett's leaning out of the car window with a mischievous grin. I grab my bag and quickly leave the house. As I climb into the car, Scarlett gives me an exaggerated wink. "So, spill the beans, girl! What happened last night?"

I roll my eyes and playfully nudge her shoulder. "Nothing!" I protest, perhaps a bit too forcefully. "Eric and I just had a pleasant evening together."

She raises an eyebrow, clearly not convinced. "Pleasant evening, huh? Well, I'll let you off the hook for now. By the way, cute dress."

I hesitate for a moment, then blush and admit, "Well... we sort of... spent the night together."

My body jolts forward as she exclaims, "Do what! Oh my gosh!"

I chuckle, trying to keep the mood light. "Can you not slam on the brakes, please!"

"Sorry, sorry!" She looks at the road, her mouth curving into a smile. "Sex is a big deal for you. You wouldn't have given your virginity up for just anyone."

"I know. Something about him just feels..." I trail off.

"Right?"

"Yes."

I chuckle. As we drive back to my place, I can't help but think about Eric's note and the small gestures that make him so endearing. I've never felt this way about someone, and it's a delightful feeling.

Scarlett drops me off, allowing me to come in a little late since I stayed over at Eric's. I stand in front of my closet, trying to decide what to wear for the day ahead. After a few moments of contemplation, I settle on a navy-blue blouse and a pair of well-fitted blue jeans. It's a classic and professional look that will do for my barista job. I quickly slip into my outfit, smoothing out any wrinkles.

As I stand in front of the mirror, I give myself a once-over and adjust a stray strand of hair. I grab my purse and head to the café.

The café greets me with the scent of fresh coffee and a lively hum of chatter. I tie my apron on as I gear up for another day's work. Scarlett is behind the counter, cursing at the register.

"You good?" I ask.

"Yeah, this damn thing is a pain in my ass. I need to get another register, preferably all digital."

"Well, I mean, yeah, that thing is a dinosaur."

My phone buzzes, a call from Mom lighting up the screen.

"Hey, Mom, what's up?" I ask.

"Hey, any chance you could come to Lucas Law Office this afternoon? The lawyer will be here to discuss the will."

"What time?" I ask.

"2 o'clock" she says.

"Scar?" I call out.

"Yeah?" she replies, coming around the corner looking at me.

"Hey, is it alright if I clock out early? The lawyer for Ray's will is going to go over it at 2."

"Yeah, just make sure the inventory checklist is finished."

"Alright, Mom, I'll be there in a couple of hours."

I hang up and head to the back to start the inventory. My mind wanders to my mom and I think about how hard this must be for her, how alone she must feel now. Before Ray entered our lives, it always felt as if it had only been the two of us, despite my dad's presence. Because of it, we have a special bond of understanding and love. We share everything with each other, and even if we are angry at one another, we always talk it out. She's the only one who understands me; she knows what I've been through because she's been through it, too. My father isn't just abusive toward me. For years, he was and still is the same to her.

I remember I'd sit at the bottom of the stairs as a kid,

listening to my mom and dad on the phone. She'd have him on speaker, with Ray listening by her side.

"Drop the child support, and I'll pay you without a debt on my back," he says in a harsh tone.

"Paying child support is the bare minimum of your responsibility to Hailey," I hear my mom say.

"You won't even fucking try to drop child support."

"I have asked them about dropping it. They will not. And if you can easily pay without a debt on your back, you wouldn't have an issue paying with it!" my mom screams through the phone, her voice cracking and a cough following.

"Go to hell!" he says.

There was silence after that.

"Ugh, I fucking hate that man!" she screams.

I hurry back up the stairs and into my room, closing the door slightly and putting my earbuds in to listen to my CD.

My mom never used the child support money for herself. It was always dedicated to helping me, whether it was for clothing, school supplies, or keeping the lights on. Her financial situation has never been great, but even if it were, my dad has consistently been a lazy individual who never bothers to find a job, not even to support his own flesh and blood.

He often boasts about having significant sums of money without disclosing their source. All the while, my mom was doing her best to raise me.

Neither of us has completely severed ties with him. Perhaps it's because my mom worries that, in case something happens to me, I might need his help. However, she also fears that he might be so self-centered that he wouldn't help me at all.

"It's about 2 o'clock. Are you heading out?" Scarlett asks, pulling me out of my memories.

I look at my watch and gasp. "Yeah, I didn't realize it

was already close to 2."

"I'll clock you out. Tell me how everything goes."

"Thank you, I will," I say, while walking out the door.

I FIND MYSELF SEATED ON THE COUCH OF LUCAS LAW Office. My mom is fidgeting beside me. The room is filled with a sense of anticipation as we wait for Mr. Lucas to read Ray's will. I have no idea what to expect from his final wishes, aside from him giving mom his truck and maybe a few items to me. Mr. Lucas clears his throat, his eyes fixed on the legal document before him.

"Thank you both for coming today. I know this is a difficult time," he starts. "As per Ray's last will and testament, I am here to distribute his assets."

"To you, Carly, Ray is giving you half a million dollars from his estate," Mr. Lucas begins.

I gasp. I can't believe my ears. My eyes fill up with tears. Half a million dollars is more than I could have ever imagined. I mean, I knew he worked a job that paid well, but not once did I ever think he had so much saved.

"And to you, Hailey," Mr. Lucas continues, his gaze shifting to me, "he has left you $200,000."

My jaw drops in astonishment. My mom looks at me, tears in her eyes. Tears stream down my cheeks, and I reach for my mom's hand, squeezing it tightly. "Ray is always taking care of us, even after he is gone," I whisper to her, my voice choking with emotion. She nods, her eyes shining with a mix of feelings.

Mr. Lucas then added, "Ray also left one car each, to both of you. The Jeep is for Hailey, knowing how much you loved working on it with him. It's a way for his memory to live on through your bond."

Mom and I exchange a knowing look. It's a bittersweet moment. A reminder of the man we had lost, but also a testament to the love he had for us in his own unique way.

"Mom, I had no idea how much he had saved," I say.

"I knew, but he didn't want you to know much because of your dad. I was afraid of what he might do," she explains.

I nod. "I understand."

"Thank you, Mr. Lucas. This has been helpful."

We shake his hand and head out of the office.

As we pull into my driveway after leaving the lawyer's office, mom looks at me and asks, "Dinner at my house in a few days?"

"Sounds good."

"How about you invite Eric? I'd love to get to know him more," she suggests.

I chuckle. "Really? You've never wanted me to bring home other guys I've dated."

"That's because they weren't as nice."

I playfully roll my eyes. "What are you making?"

"Your favorite, of course."

"Well, make sure you use the homemade pasta sauce this time. The store-bought version made me sick," I laugh.

"I won't make that mistake again," she declares. After stepping out and closing the car door, I watch her wave as she drives off.

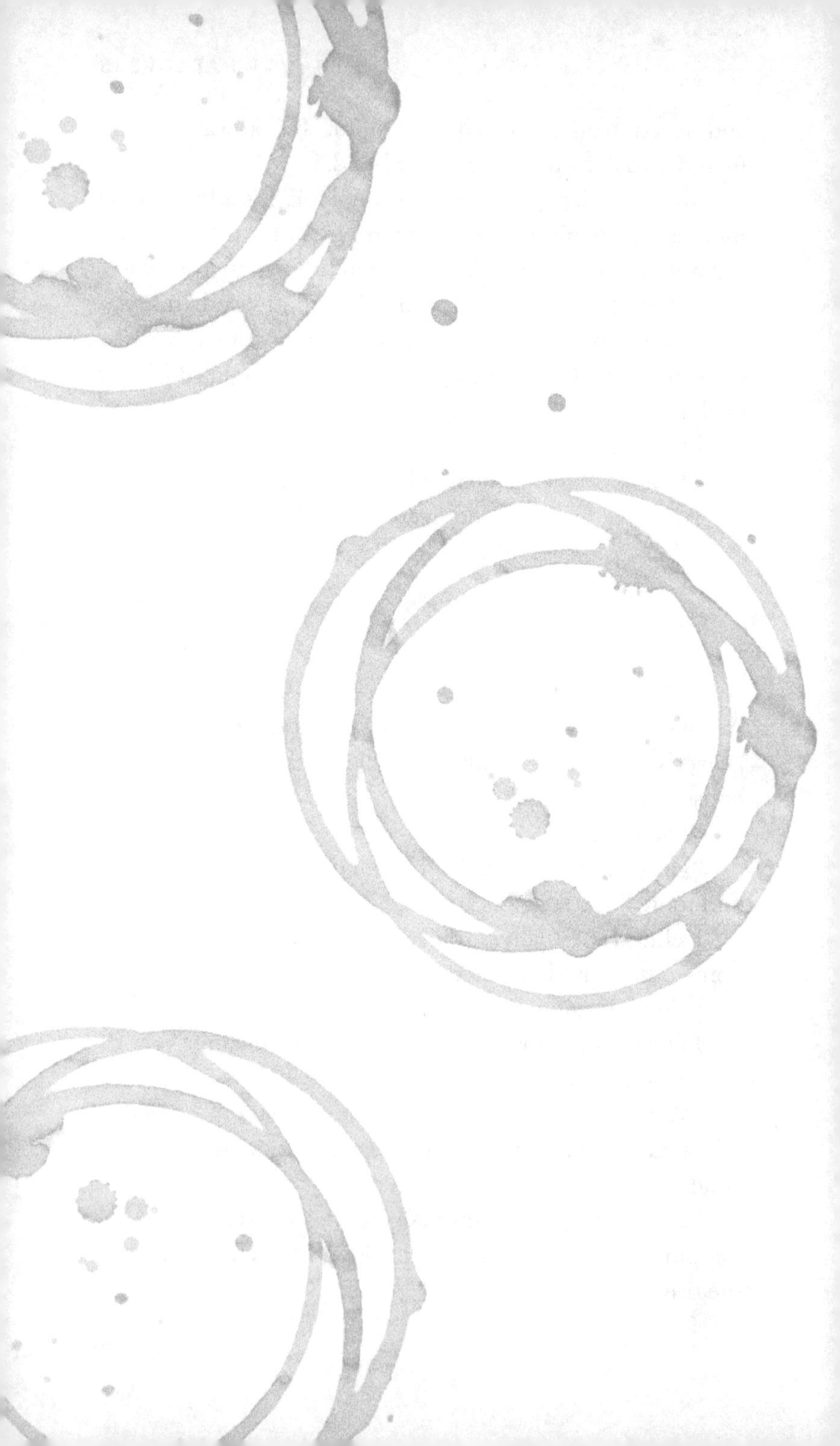

CHAPTER TWENTY-ONE

I SIGH, LYING BACK ON MY BED, THINKING ABOUT THE NEWS I just received. I pull my phone from the charger and unlock it, tapping Eric's name.

ME

How about dinner at my mom's soon?
She's invited you.

After about a minute, I see three dots on the screen that tell me he's typing.

ERIC

Count me in!

ME

I'll text you the date and time.

ERIC

See you then, beautiful.

I decide to call Scarlett.
"Hey, how did everything go?" she asks.

"Good! We'll discuss it during our movie night this weekend, but you're going to be pleasantly surprised," I reply.

"Well, whatever it is, I'm sure it's good!"

"My mom wants me to invite Eric to dinner soon."

"Oh, what'd you say?" she asks.

"Yes…"

"You're so smitten over him. I love it!"

"I know, he's just so…" I trail off.

"Gentlemanly?"

"Yeah, more than any other guy I've dated."

"I believe it," she says.

"What do you mean?"

"I mean, I've never seen you smile with others the way you do with him."

"Do you think these feelings are too sudden?" I ask.

"If it feels right, I don't think so."

"Talk soon?"

"Love you, Boo," she responds, hanging up.

EVERY SINGLE BONE IN MY BODY WANTS HIM. IT'S LIKE HE has this spell over me, this hold. When he looks at me, all I feel is goosebumps, but my heart is also calmer around Eric than with any other man I've dated. My mom tells me that's a sign of someone being "the one."

I've spent countless nights lying awake, replaying our conversations and reliving the moments we've shared. It's as if each word he speaks has a way of imprinting itself deep on my soul, creating a connection that goes beyond the surface. His laughter is my melody, and his smile is the sun breaking through the darkest of my clouds.

How can someone ignite such a fierce longing within me and, at the same time, make me feel safe and understood? Perhaps my mom is right. Maybe the calmness I feel in his presence is a sign that he's the missing piece I've been searching for. It's not about the fireworks that explode upon every encounter, though that is there, too. Rather, the steady warmth that radiates when our eyes meet.

Tying my hair up into a high ponytail, I take one last look in the mirror, make a silly, kissy face, and laugh. I head out the door and leave to pick up Eric for dinner with my mom.

As the sun dips below the horizon, Eric and I pull into the driveway. Our relationship has yet to be officially labeled, but the undeniable connection between us is electric. He takes my hand, and as we enter my mom's house, the familiar scent of lavender fills the air.

With a charming smile, Eric extends a bouquet of pink roses for my mother.

"Thank you, Eric. These are beautiful." She excuses herself, disappearing into the kitchen to find a vase for the flowers.

Alone in the cozy living room, Eric and I settle into the plush couch, surrounded by memories of Ray.

"I remember my mischievous childhood, how I used to sneakily raid Ray's lunch box as soon as he'd return from work, nabbing his leftover snacks."

Eric chuckles. "Sounds like you were quite the little snack bandit."

I laugh. "Oh, I definitely was."

Just then, mom calls out, "Hailey, Eric, dinner is ready."

My stomach growls as she speaks those words. Eric raises a brow, smirking. "Damn girl, did you eat at all today?"

"Shut up." I laugh. He stands up and grabs my hand, helping me up before we head to the kitchen. Eric pulls out a chair, gesturing for me to sit.

I smile gratefully. "Thank you."

"So, Eric, tell me a little bit about yourself," my mom starts, her voice laced with curiosity as she pours herself a glass of wine. Her inquisitive nature is something I've grown up with, but I can't help but feel a pang of sympathy for Eric.

"Well, I'm originally from here, but I moved away when I was ten," he responds, taking a bite of his food.

I try to catch his eye, offering an encouraging smile as my mom gears up for her interrogation.

"What made your family move?" she prods, leaning forward slightly.

"My dad passed away in a boating accident. My mom needed a fresh start, so we moved," he shares, though I can sense the underlying sadness in his voice.

"I'm so sorry for your loss," I express my condolences.

"It's alright," he replies.

"Are you currently employed?" she continues with her questions, and internally, I can't help but sigh. Here we go.

"Yes, I'm a construction worker," Eric replies, maintaining his composure.

"Ah, my father was one as well." My mom nods,

placing her fork down as if she's settling in for a serious conversation. "What made you move back to Beaufort?"

Eric takes a sip of his Pepsi, momentarily breaking eye contact with my mom. "The last construction business I was working for cut everyone's hours. A buddy of mine happened to be opening up the same business here, with better hours and better pay. I decided to leave that job and come here for a fresh start."

"Sounds like it worked out for you," my mom says, her tone softening.

Eric turns his head toward me, and a warmth spreads through me at the smile he offers. "It sure did," he responds, his eyes locking onto mine.

I can feel the blood rushing to my cheeks, and I lower my gaze, taking a bite of my spaghetti to hide my growing grin.

Despite my mom's relentless questioning, the evening is going better than I had expected. As I steal glances at him between bites of my food, I can't help but be struck by how perfectly he fits into this moment, into my world. Eric's fingers brush against mine under the table, a silent show of support that makes me feel stronger. Despite the challenges ahead, having him by my side gives me a newfound sense of courage. As I savor the last bites of my dinner, I glance over at Eric, who is finishing his with a contented smile.

With the plates emptied, he stands from his seat and begins to collect not only his plate but also mine and my mom's. "I'll take care of these," Eric says.

As he disappears into the kitchen, the sound of running water and clinking dishes fill the background, a comforting lullaby to our conversation. Mom leans over and whispers in my ear, "He's a keeper, Hailey."

I nod, unable to hold back a smile. "I think so, too."

After a few minutes, Eric walks back into the dining

room, and I stand up from the table. "I'm afraid I've got to go home, Mom. I've got to work early in the morning. Thanks for dinner," I explain, seeing it's already nine in the evening.

My mom walks toward me and gives me a hug. "Love you," she says.

"Love you, too," I reply, hugging her back. We pull away, and she walks to Eric.

"May I have a hug?" she asks him.

Eric embraces my mother, and he has a smile on his face before they pull away.

"Have a good night, you two. Don't do anything I wouldn't do!"

"*Mom!*"

"What?" she asks, shooing me away.

I roll my eyes and chuckle.

"Have a good night," Eric says, and we head back to my car.

ERIC AND I STAND ON MY FRONT PORCH, BATHED IN THE soft glow of the porch light. We've been standing here for about five minutes, neither of us quite ready to say good-bye. The dinner with my mom had gone better than I could have hoped for, and the connection between me and Eric has deepened throughout the evening.

His blue eyes meet mine, and there's a warmth in his gaze that sends goosebumps over my skin. "Tonight was amazing," he finally says, breaking the silence. His soft voice, carrying a note of sincerity, making my heart flutter.

A smile tugs at the corners of my lips. "It really was. Thank you for coming."

He takes a step closer, his presence enveloping me. "Thank you for inviting me. I'm glad I got to know your mom a bit more and spend time with you."

My fingers itch to reach out and touch him, to bridge the remaining gap between us. There's an undeniable pull, a magnetic force drawing us together.

"Eric," I begin, my voice barely above a whisper, "I want you to know that… I'm really glad you're in my life."

He reaches out, his fingers gently cupping my cheek. He leans in, closing the distance between us, and our lips meet in a sweet, lingering kiss.

As we pull away, our breaths mingling, Eric smiles, his eyes filled with affection. "I'm glad, too, Hailey."

He gives my hand a gentle squeeze and turns to head down the porch steps.

"How are you getting home?" I ask.

"I'm going to walk."

"Are you sure? I can drive you," I say.

"I'll be okay."

We stare at each other for a moment, and he walks back to me, pressing his lips against mine. My heart beats faster as I deepen the kiss.

I break away to unlock the front door and we rush inside. I drop my purse, and he lifts me up, his hands gentle, yet firm, grabbing my ass. Eric takes us into my room and turns on the lamp. The soft glow casts a warm and intimate ambiance. He gently guides me to the bed and lays me down as my heart pounds against my chest.

As he stands before me, he unbuttons his shirt, revealing the sculpted contours of his chest. The sight of him shirtless sends a shiver down my spine, and I can't seem to tear my eyes away. Feeling a surge of boldness, I reach out and unbuckle his belt. The sound of the clasp releasing echoes in the quiet room. My fingers tremble slightly as I slide the belt off him, the anticipation of what lies ahead making my pulse race.

Our eyes lock. As he steps closer, he brushes a lock of hair from my face, his touch sending electric sparks through me. Our lips meet once again, this time with the hunger that has been growing steadily throughout the evening.

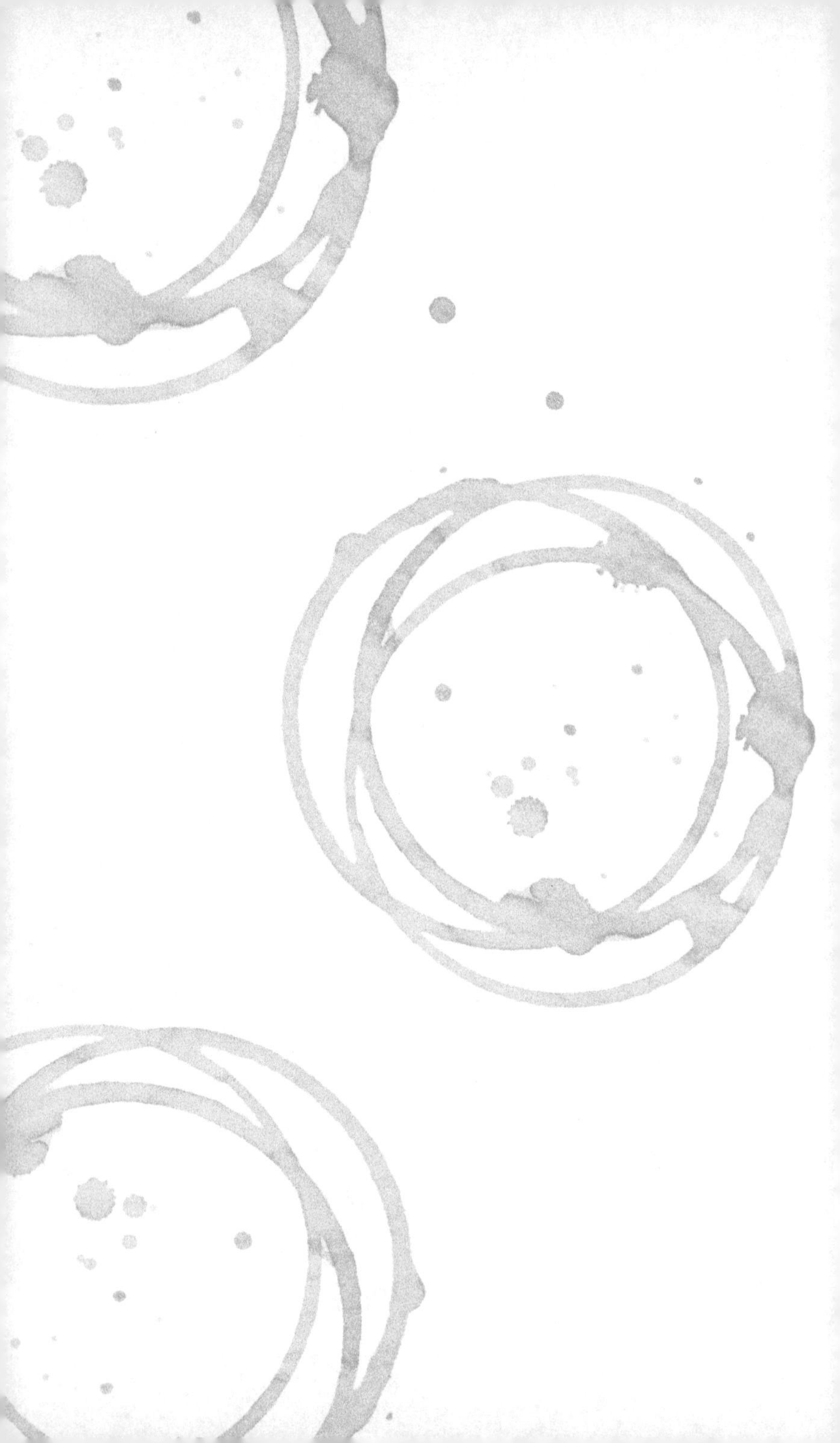

CHAPTER TWENTY-TWO

THE NEXT MORNING, I STIR FROM A PEACEFUL SLUMBER TO the smell of pancakes wafting through the air. The delicious scent wraps around me like a warm embrace, coaxing me out of my dreams and into the day. Groggily, I stretch and take in the soft morning light filtering through the curtains.

The rhythmic sizzle of batter hitting a hot pan is a comforting sound. Eric is so absorbed in his cooking that he hasn't noticed me yet. I watch in silent appreciation as he skillfully maneuvers the spatula under the pancake, a look of concentration on his face. There is something incredibly endearing about the way he approaches even the simplest of tasks with care and dedication. Finally, unable to contain my smile any longer, I clear my throat. Eric turns, his eyes lighting up as he sees me.

"Good morning, gorgeous," he says, his voice warm and filled with affection.

"Good morning," I reply, crossing the distance between us.

Without a word, he reaches out and pulls me into his arms, holding me close as we share a sweet morning kiss.

"Are you my morning chef now?" I joke.

He lets out a laugh. "If you want me to be, yes."

"Mmm, you already are at this point. I don't see a reason to stop now."

"I'm not complaining." He grabs a plate of food and hands it to me with a fork, syrup, and butter already added.

"Can I have a glass of orange juice, chef?" I smirk.

"You sure can." While he pours the juice, someone knocks on the front door. I check my phone, and it's only 6 AM.

When I open the front door, my eyes widen at the sight of my father.

His hands are stuffed in his pockets, his face red. Finally, he breaks the silence, his words dripping with bitterness. "So, you're living the high life now, aren't you? Thanks to that inheritance."

I gulp. "How did you find out about that?"

"Doesn't matter. Can we have a civil conversation?" he asks.

"With you? That's unlikely," I snap.

"Don't speak to me that way. I'm your dad."

"I don't care who you are. This is my house. I choose who I will and will not talk to." I struggle to find my voice, to defend myself against him.

His anger only intensifies. "I have paid child support since the divorce. You fucking owe me!"

"You should've signed your rights away if you didn't want to agree to pay child support!" I yell.

"You're right, I should have. I should have kept telling your whore of a mother that you weren't mine. Because you're not."

"If I wasn't yours, I wouldn't look like a twin of my grandmother, or like your sister, or have your ears or temper. You always say this to piss my mom off! You were never there for me, Dad! You were never a real father. You were selfish and absent. You treat me like crap and call me every fucking name in the book. What the fuck is wrong with you?"

Eric steps in front of me.

I can see the shock on my dad's face. He didn't expect me to have company.

"Get off the property," Eric says calmly but sternly.

"Who the fuck are you to tell me what I should and shouldn't do? This isn't any of your business," my dad yells in his face with spit flying out of his mouth.

Eric's voice takes on an even colder edge. His eyes lock onto my father's with unwavering determination. "I don't care whose business it is. What I do care about is your daughter's well-being. Now, I'm going to give you a choice: leave peacefully or I'll make sure you do."

My dad's face contorts with anger, his fists clenching and unclenching at his sides. I can see the conflict in his eyes, the struggle between his pride and anger. With one swift move, he swings his fist into Eric's face, knocking him back a little.

My eyes widen, and before I can react, Eric tackles him to the ground, pinning his hands behind his back.

"Call the police, now!" Eric yells to me while keeping my dad pinned.

My breath hitches while I run into the house and dial 911.

"911, what's your emergency?"

"Hello, my dad just punched my boyfriend in the face, and now they are fighting."

"Ma'am, what's the address of your emergency?"

Before I can say it, my phone dies. *Shit.* I quickly plug it in, then head straight to my neighbor's across the street. Panic surges through me as I frantically knock on the door. Time feels like it's crawling, and I hope someone will answer and offer assistance. My heart pounds in my chest, and my mind races.

Seconds turn into an eternity, but finally, the door opens. Sarah's eyes widen as she takes in the chaotic scene unfolding in front of her.

"What's going on?" she asks.

"My dad and boyfriend are fighting," I manage to blurt out, my voice trembling.

Sarah nods, and without hesitation, rushes back inside to call the police.

I return to my front yard to find Eric still holding my dad down, both of them breathing heavily from the struggle.

The sirens blare louder as two police cars pull up. Two officers get out and pull Eric off my dad.

"Fuck you and your slut of a girlfriend!" my dad screams while being handcuffed.

My heart shatters into a million pieces and falls into the pit of my stomach. I can't control it anymore. I burst into tears. I turn and see Eric also getting arrested. Through the tears, I look at the cop handcuffing him. "Sir, please don't do that. My boyfriend was only defending himself and me. I have video footage of everything."

The officer looks at me. "May we see it?"

I nod, gesturing for them to follow me into the house.

THE OFFICER STANDS BEHIND ME AS I LOG INTO MY security camera app on the computer and show him the footage from beginning to end. I can't watch it and look away until it's over. When the video is complete, the officer asks a few questions about what happened to make sure the video didn't miss anything.

"Do you want to press charges?" he asks us, writing notes down on his notepad.

I hesitate, looking at Eric with questioning eyes. Eric sees my distress and asks, "Do you not want me to press charges?"

I take a deep breath and shake my head. "I think we need to. I don't like that he hurt you, and he needs to learn that I will do anything to protect the people I care about."

The officer nods. "Alright, we'll press charges for the assault. If you ever feel unsafe, or need assistance in the future, don't hesitate to call us. That's what we're here for."

"Thank you. Is he going to jail?" I ask.

"We are going to bring him down to the station for more questions." The cop offers a reassuring smile and turns to leave. As he walks away, I'm left sitting on my chair, my heart still heavy with the emotional turmoil of the morning. Eric closes the door and takes my hand.

"We'll get through this," he says, squeezing my hand. "We'll figure things out together."

I manage a weak smile, grateful for his support. "I hope so."

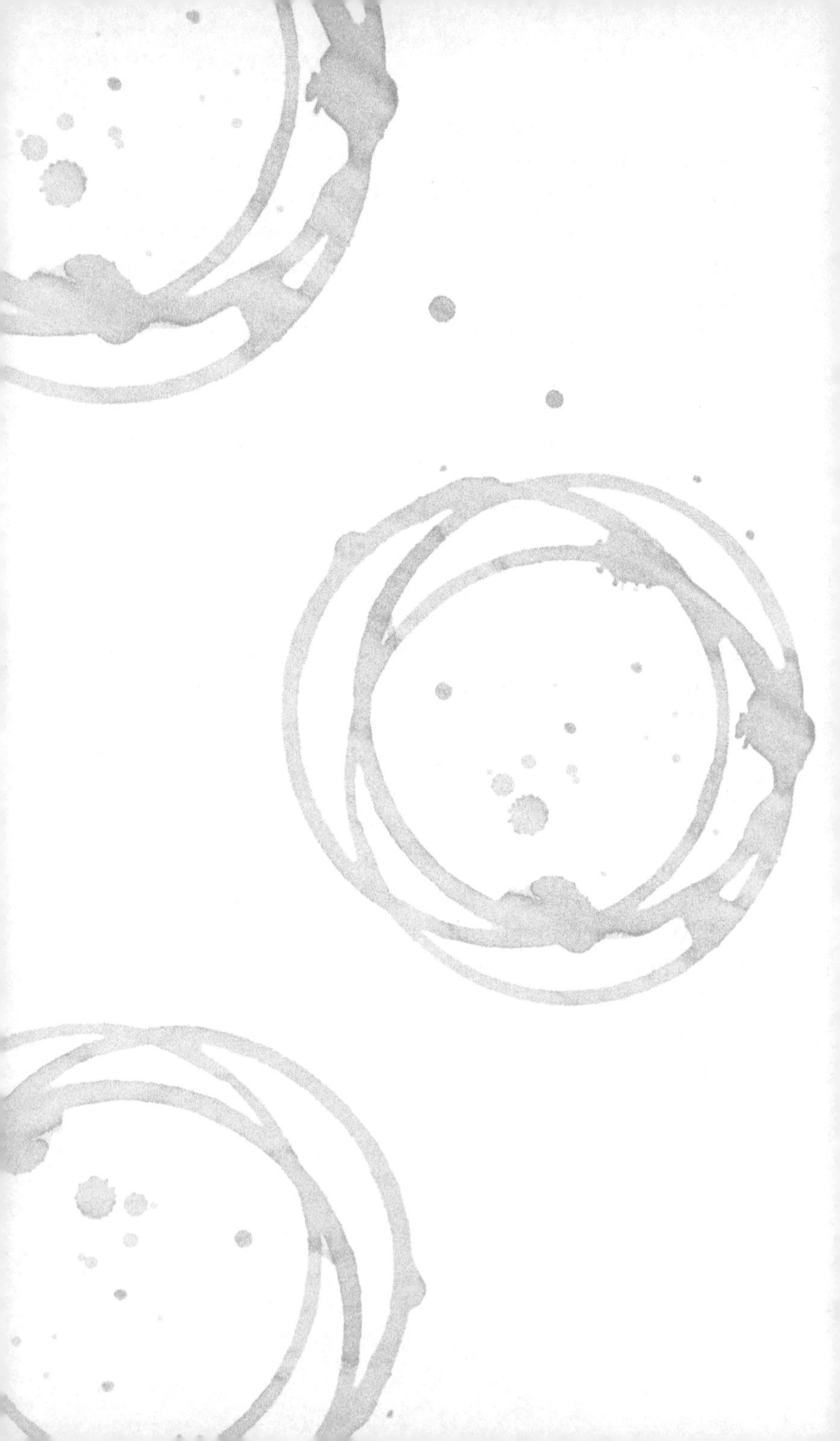

CHAPTER TWENTY-THREE

I can't shake the chill that has settled deep within me after the events on my front lawn. My fingers tremble as I tap my mother's name in my phone. She's the only person who will understand the tangled mess my life has become.

The phone rings, and her gentle voice answers. "Hi, honey."

"Mom," I whisper, the word catching in my throat.

"What's wrong, darling? You sound so… distraught."

I take a deep breath, trying to find the strength to put my thoughts into words.

"It's Dad. He showed up at my doorstep, and things got ugly. I don't know how he found out, but he knew about the money I got from Ray's will and he kept saying that I owed him. Eric got hurt, and the cops showed up, and now Dad's going to jail."

A heavy silence follows, broken only by the faint sound of my mother's ragged breathing. I can picture her holding the phone, her face filled with worry and guilt. "I'm sorry, honey. I might have let it slip during one of our fights that

Ray left you money," she finally says, her voice trembling. Tears well up in my eyes, but I blink them back. "I love you."

"I love you, too, sweetheart. Now, try to get some rest. I'll handle everything from here."

With those words, she hangs up the phone, leaving me with a sense of fragile hope that maybe, just maybe, things can finally start to get better.

I sit down beside Eric on the couch and hand him a bag of peas. He presses them to his face with one hand and wraps the other around my shoulders, pulling me close. I can feel the tension in his muscles, a reflection of the worry that has etched lines onto his face. "Are you okay?" he asks, his voice gentle but filled with concern.

I sigh, leaning into his comforting embrace. "I can't seem to catch a break. I think I just need to take the day off. I don't think I can focus at work with all of this going on in my head."

Understanding, he nods. "Take all the time you need, Hailey. I'm here for you, and I know Scarlett is, too."

I pulled out my phone and dial Scarlett's number.

"Hey, what's up?"

"Hey, " I begin, my voice shaky but determined. "I won't be able to make it to work today. My father showed up on my doorstep this morning, and I need to sort some things out."

Concern laces Scarlett's response. "Oh no. Is everything okay?"

"It's just a temporary thing, I hope. My dad found out

about me getting some money from Ray and showed up at my house. A fight broke out between Eric and my dad, and I just need to take a breather," I say.

Scarlett's tone softens. "Don't worry about work. Take all the time you need. I'll manage here, and you can update me when you're ready."

"Thank you."

The weight of the world seems to press down on me as I hang up the phone. Eric tightens his arms around me, pulling me closer, his silent presence a comforting reminder that I'm not alone in this storm.

I lean my head against his chest, my fingers tracing aimless patterns on his shirt. "Eric," I whisper, my voice heavy with uncertainty, "do you think I'm making the right choice, taking a day off?"

Eric gently tilts my chin up to meet his gaze. His warm blue eyes hold nothing but unwavering support. "Hailey, it's been a rough week. You deserve a break."

I nod, but even with his reassurance, doubt gnaws at the edges of my mind. I have always been the one who keeps everything together, who pushes through whatever life throws my way. Now, I feel like I am falling apart.

"Don't you need to go to work?" I ask, my voice still quivering.

He sighs, running a hand through his tousled hair, clearly torn between his responsibilities and his concern for me. "I do," he admits. "I'm not able to call off this week."

I nod, understanding the practicality of his situation. "I'll be okay here," I assure him, though my confidence wavers.

"You sure?" Eric asks one more time, his eyes searching mine for any sign of doubt.

"Yes," I say, mustering as much conviction as I can. I

know I have to face the turmoil in my life head-on, and this is a moment to prove it to myself.

With a tender kiss on my forehead, Eric reluctantly heads toward the door. "Call me if you need anything, okay?"

"I will," I say, watching him go, a mixture of emotions churning inside me.

SCROLLING THROUGH MY PHONE, I SMILE AT THE FUNNY videos and cute photos of Scarlett on social media. I tap her name, sending her a message.

ME

Hey, dinner Thursday?

I look at the clock and notice it's already 3 PM. My gosh, it felt like 6 AM was five minutes ago.

While waiting for Scar to respond, I go to exit the message app when I see my dad's old texts underneath hers. With a shaky thumb, I tap them open and scroll all the way from the beginning, reading everything he's ever said to me, recalling where I was and what I was doing during each message he sent.

DAD

I hate you and your mother, go to hell.

My dad's hurtful words echoed as I diligently wiped down the coffee-stained tables at work. Customers walked past, oblivious to the sadness inside me as I discreetly checked my phone.

DAD

Do I really have to pay child support just to
have a relationship with you? That's
fucked up.

His hateful words flashed across my screen while I sat at my mom's table with her and Ray. I chose not to react, keeping these hurtful messages to myself.

DAD

What do I need to do to fix our relationship?

Another message while I was in the tub, bubbles all around, and a fruity drink in hand, my attempt to escape the stress of work over-shadowed by the ongoing emotional turmoil caused by my dad's verbal abuse.

My phone pings, snapping me from my thoughts.

SCARLETT

See you then. I'll bring ice cream!

I smile and place my phone down, then doze off to sleep.

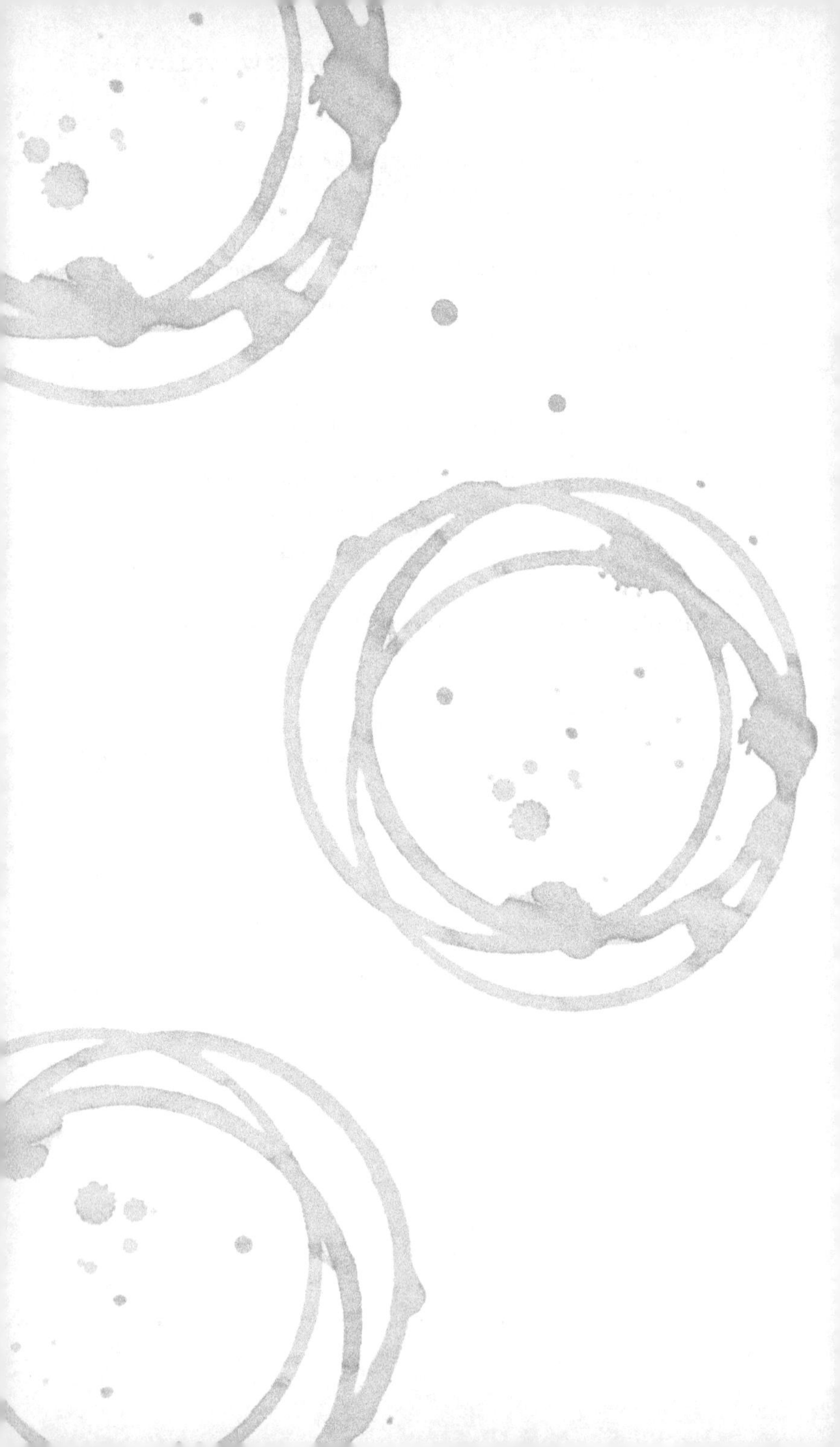

CHAPTER TWENTY-FOUR

Thursday has arrived, and I'm suddenly roused from my slumber by a sharp knock at my door. As I regain consciousness, I notice that the sun has set, and the moon now dominates the night sky. Groggily, I reach for my phone, unlocking it to check the time: 7:50 PM.

I can't believe it; I've slept the entire day away. I notice a text from Scarlett, saying she is on her way, that was sent 10 minutes ago.

I place my phone back on the coffee table, drag myself off the couch, and rub my tired eyes as I make my way to the front door.

"Hey," Scarlett says with a genuine smile. "I brought the ice cream, just like I promised."

"I'm sorry, I didn't order or make any dinner."

"It's okay, we can order something."

She carries the ice cream to my kitchen and places it in the freezer with a sense of familiarity, a routine we've repeated countless times. Then she opens the fridge and retrieves a bottle of wine. After pouring two small glasses, Scarlett heads into the living room, where I've managed to pull myself together enough to sit down. She hands me a glass and takes a seat beside me on the couch.

Scarlett's eyes are filled with concern as she asks softly, "How are you doing, Hailey? I haven't seen much of you in the last few days. I've missed our time together and want to catch up."

Tears overflow from the corners of my eyes as I pour my heart out to her, recounting every painful detail of what has unfolded. Her face appears calm, yet beneath the surface, I detect an intense blaze in her eyes. She understands all too well the depths of my father's cruelty and the scars he's inflicted upon me.

She places her drink down, her frustration boiling over. "What the hell is wrong with him? I'm so sorry, Hailey, but I absolutely despise that man."

I simply nod, my tears breaking free and streaming down my face. Her eyes soften, and she engulfs me in a tight embrace. "I love you, baby girl," she whispers.

"It's just not fair for me to have to sit through the pain he's caused," I manage to say, my voice trembling.

Without hesitation, she springs into action. "I'm getting us some Oreo cookie ice cream, and we're going to watch a movie. I'll also order pizza," she says as she rises from the couch.

"That's exactly why you're my best friend," I reply, a small laugh escaping my lips.

"Never forget it!"

Scar hands me a bowl of ice cream, sitting next to me once again. As I scoop up a spoonful, I can't help but wonder about the idea of visiting my dad, to talk with him, confront him maybe. It's a notion that lingers in the back of my mind. A part of me yearns for closure, to confront him and demand answers. But another part fears what I might uncover if I delve into the depths of his twisted mind.

As we settle in for our movie night, my mind remains consumed by thoughts of my father. The wounds he's inflicted on my heart still ache, and the fire in my friend's eyes mirrors the burning anger within me.

I share my thoughts with Scar. "You know, I've been thinking about confronting him."

She turns to me, concern etched on her face. "Are you sure that's a good idea? I mean, after everything he's done…"

I pause, weighing the pros and cons. "I know it's risky, and there's a chance it could make things even messier, but part of me just needs to confront him, to make him see the pain he's caused. Maybe… just maybe it could bring some sort of closure."

She squeezes my hand reassuringly. "I understand. Just promise me you'll think about it more before making a decision. Your well-being is what matters most."

I smile gratefully. "Thank you. You're always looking out for me. Let's focus on our movie night for now, and we'll deal with the rest when the time is right."

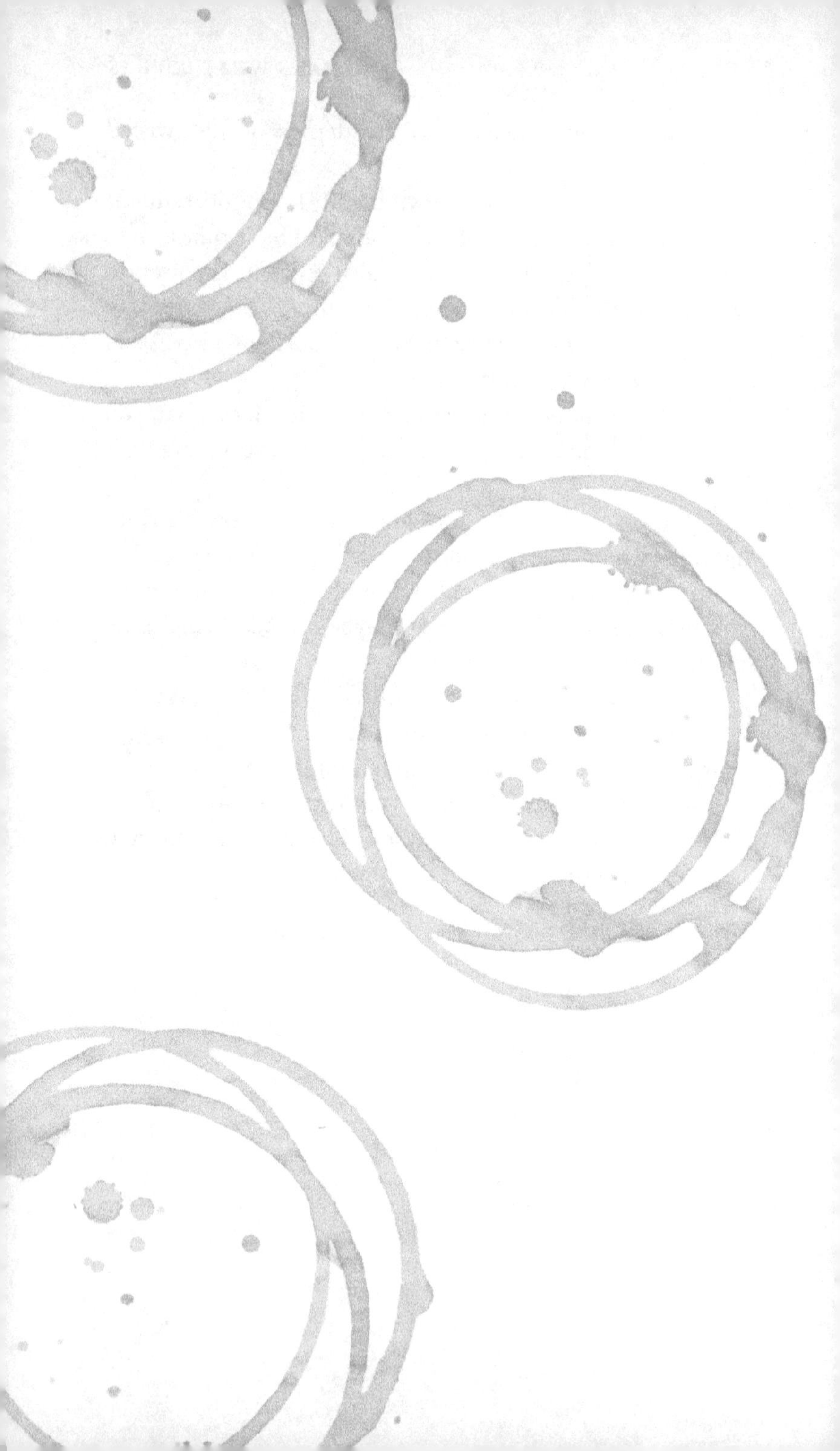

CHAPTER TWENTY-FIVE

"Ah, goodness, that's hot!" I say as coffee spills on my jeans.

"You alright?" Scar asks, emerging from around the corner.

"Yeah, I'm fine, just thankful I chose to wear jeans today!" I rush to the bathroom, grabbing some paper towels to clean up the coffee as much as I can.

"Speaking of today," Scar starts, "are you ready for game night tonight?"

I nod, still nursing my coffee-soaked jeans. "Absolutely! It's been a while since our last one. Any new games in mind?"

"Maybe," Scar replies nonchalantly.

"Well, our old favorites never disappoint."

"And the prize this time will be free coffee for the rest of the summer."

"No five-hundred-dollar prize this time?"

Scar lets out a hearty laugh. "We can't make it too easy, can we?"

"If you say so." I laugh.

I return to the register, still a bit preoccupied with thoughts about yesterday's incident with my dad and Eric. It's hard to shake off the worry and guilt that gnaws at me, but I try to focus on the upcoming game night to lighten my mood. I pull out my phone, tapping Eric's name and sending him a text.

ME

Hey, you okay? Haven't heard from you since yesterday morning.

He seems like such a good man. I'm hoping my dad didn't make him change his mind about dating me.

He doesn't respond, and I stuff my phone into my back pocket and focus on work.

THE HOURS PASS SLOWLY, BUT EVENTUALLY, IT'S TIME TO prepare for game night. Scar and I set up the cozy corner near the back, arranging board games, card decks, and a stack of our favorite tabletop games. The soft glow of fairy lights adds a touch of magic to the atmosphere, creating a warm and inviting space for our friends.

I look at Scar as I clean up the tables. "What's the plan for tonight?"

"Well, they can bring a couple of their own games, but those who didn't will grab a stack from here, and we will make sure everyone has the same number of games. And as usual, the first table to go through all games wins a prize," she says.

As our customers start to arrive, the energy in the room

shifts from the mundane routines of daily life to the excitement of friendly competition and laughter. Sam, the resident board game enthusiast, arrives with a bag full of strategy games. Lisa and Max, the couple who won last time and always bring delicious homemade snacks, enter with a tray of freshly baked cookies and a bowl of their famous guacamole.

I unlock my phone, tap the play button on the music app, and glance up as the rhythmic beat flows through the speakers. Tonight promises to be a blast. I take a quick survey of the tables to ensure everyone has the five games they need.

"Let the games begin!" Scar's voice booms through the wireless microphone she's wielding.

The atmosphere becomes electric as everyone eagerly delves into their first game.

I retreat behind the counter, settling into my chair. I scroll through my phone, anxiously checking for a reply from Eric, but there's nothing.

"I'm sure everything is okay," Scar reassures me, appearing by my side and placing a comforting hand on my shoulder.

I can't help but express my concerns, my voice tinged with uncertainty. "What if he was too good to be true?"

Scar, in a surprising display of seriousness, responds, "If that's the case, I'll personally take care of him for you."

I shake my head and laugh.

"What? I'm serious," she says, a hand on her hip.

"I know you would, that's what makes it funny."

The night buzzes with lively conversations, laughter, and a contagious sense of enjoyment. Some individuals at the same table are particularly enthusiastic, displaying a competitive spirit that adds to the excitement.

Suddenly, a woman shouts, "BINGO!" The room

erupts in cheers and celebration as Scar announces, "We have a WINNER!"

I glance up from serving a muffin and join in the jubilation, shouting, "Woo!"

The triumphant player rises from her seat and makes her way to Scar. Grinning, she expresses her gratitude, saying, "Thank you for these game nights; they're incredibly entertaining!"

"You're welcome!" Scar says, handing her a certificate for free coffee for the rest of the summer.

"Let's all get a selfie," I say to them both.

"Heck yes, please!" the girl says.

I grab my phone, and we huddle close together.

"Say cheese!" Scar says.

"Cheese!" we all say.

I place my phone back into my pocket.

"I'm so glad you came! See you back soon?" Scar asks.

"Of course!" she says.

On game nights like this one, we usually leave the café open until someone emerges victorious. As the final customer bids us farewell and I lock the door, I give them a friendly wave and turn to help Scarlett clean up the dining area.

"Another successful game night," I say with a satisfied smile, starting to clear away the empty cups and plates from the tables.

Scarlett nods in agreement, her eyes reflecting the warm ambiance of the café. The lingering laughter and conversations of our happy customers still resonate in the cozy atmosphere.

"Definitely! Everyone seemed to have a great time tonight. The chocolate fondue you made was a big hit, too," Scarlett says.

I chuckle as I continue tidying up. "I'm glad they enjoyed it. It's always nice to see our customers having fun. By the way, did you notice if anyone was close to winning any of the games?"

Scarlett looks around the café, then shakes her head. "I'm not sure. I was mainly focused on keeping the drinks and snacks flowing. But I can check the scorecards and see if anyone was close to victory." Scarlett returns with the scorecards in hand and begins going through them. "It looks like a few games were pretty close. Some regulars were just one move away from winning in that intense chess match. And in the card game corner, it seems like the game of 'Uno' was heating up, too."

"Well, that's the beauty of game night; it keeps everyone engaged and entertained. Let's note down those close calls so we can congratulate the winners next time."

Scarlett finishes gathering the scorecards and smiles. "Absolutely. Game night is a big part of what makes this café so special."

We both finish cleaning up the dining area, and as I glance around one last time, I can't help but agree.

The café is more than just a place to grab a coffee or play board games; it's a gathering place for friends, old and new, to share laughter and good times.

With everything in order, Scarlett and I prepare to close up shop for the night, already looking forward to the next game night at our beloved café.

Turning into my driveway, raindrops dance on my windshield. My breath quickens with every step I take toward the porch, where the man I've missed so dearly sits, sheltering himself from the pouring rain. I can't shake the flutter of hope in my heart. Lightning streaks across the darkened sky, illuminating his tousled brown hair and tanned skin.

Eric. The name plays like a melody in my soul, and the moment our eyes meet, it's as if the world holds its breath, waiting for our reunion. The thunder rumbles in the distance, mirroring the racing of my own heart.

My entire body trembles, and I stand before him like a fragile leaf. The rain pours down relentlessly, but nothing can dampen the warmth that spreads through me as I close the distance between us. I can't help but laugh, feeling the cold droplets of rain soaking through my clothes.

The porch light creates a soft, golden halo around Eric, making his blue eyes sparkle like the sun glistening on the ocean waves. His smile is a welcome sight. Eric stands, his arms outstretched, and we embrace in a tight, fervent hug that speaks volumes without words. We hold each other, the rain serving as a backdrop to our reunion, washing away the time we've spent apart.

"I've missed you," I whisper into his ear, my voice barely audible over the patter of raindrops.

"I've missed you, too, more than words can say," Eric replies, his voice filled with emotion. He pulls back slightly, cupping my face in his hands, his thumbs brushing away rain-soaked strands of hair that cling to my skin.

"Why didn't you respond to my text?" I whisper. My heart aches with the fear that I had somehow driven him away, that I had messed everything up.

He doesn't answer immediately. His eyes lock onto mine and his lips part, as if searching for the right words.

"Did I do something wrong?" I ask.

Eric's gaze never leaves me, his expression a mixture of understanding and something deeper. His shoulders slump as if the weight of the world rests on them, and finally, he says, "No, Hailey. It's not you. It was never you."

His words hang in the air, mingling with the raindrops, and I take a step closer, feeling the warmth of his presence. He continues, his voice soft, "I had to sort out my own feelings. It's complicated, but one thing I'm sure of is how much I care about you."

Tears well up in my eyes as I listen to him, his vulnerability stripping away any doubts I carry. I take a deep breath, feeling the weight of my own secrets pressing down on me. It's time to be honest.

"I need to tell you something," I admit, my voice shaking with raw emotion. "I've been afraid to fully commit to a relationship because of my past, because of my unresolved issues with my father."

Eric reaches out and gently wipes away a tear that escapes my eye, his touch as soft as his understanding. "Hailey," he says, his voice filled with sincerity. "I promise you, I'll stand by your side. We can face your past and your fears together. I care about you more than I can express."

The weight I've carried for so long lifts, and I lean into his comforting presence, feeling a newfound sense of hope. The storm that has been raging within me finally starts to subside.

As the rain continues its relentless downpour, he tenderly cups my face, his eyes shimmering with an intensity that tugs at the deepest recesses of my heart. Without a single word, he closes the gap between us, his lips meeting mine in a kiss so profound, so raw, that it feels like the answer to every question I'd ever dared to ask.

With our hearts beautifully entwined, we are ready to

confront whatever challenges lay ahead, prepared to make each other's hearts flutter in pure, unadulterated happiness, knowing beyond a shadow of a doubt that we are meant to be together.

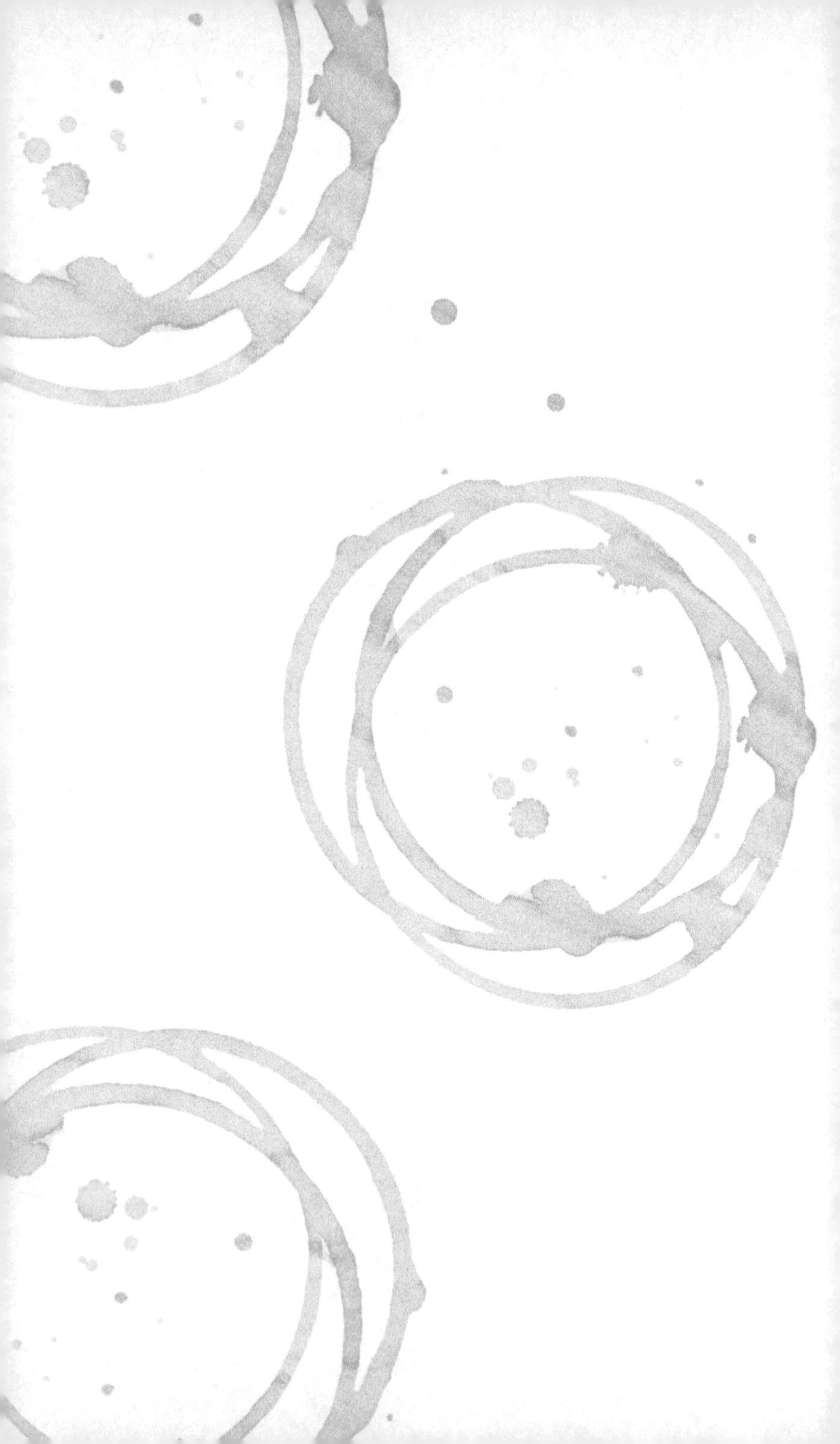

CHAPTER TWENTY-SIX

THE SUNDAY MORNING SUN STREAMS THROUGH THE curtains, casting a warm glow across the living room. Eric lays beside me on the couch, our fingers intertwined, as if the night had sealed some unspoken promise between us. After what happened last night, I can't help but feel closer to him than ever before.

I can't deny that I was afraid to open up, to let him in completely. My father's violent outburst still haunts my mind, and I know it has left its mark on Eric as well. But there is something about the way he looks at me, with understanding and empathy, that makes it easier to share my pain.

We spend the day together, just the two of us, in the sanctuary of my living room. It's as if the world outside doesn't exist, and it's just the two of us, trying to piece together our broken lives. As we talk, I find myself telling him more about my past, about the fear that has gripped me for so long. Eric listens, his eyes filled with compassion, never pressing me for details I'm not ready to share.

It's the first time in a long while that I feel safe enough

to talk about the nightmares that haunt me. I shut myself from the emotions that always come up from times like this —hurt, anger, confusion. Whenever the memories start to cloud my mind, I push them away, not wanting to let the pain seep in.

Eric hears the hesitation in my voice and offers a way out. "How about dinner tonight? We could cook something together, or if you prefer, I can order your favorite takeout. We'll set the table, light some candles, and just enjoy each other's company."

The idea sounds enchanting, and a sense of warmth blossoms within me at the thought of sharing an intimate dinner with Eric. "I'd love to," I reply. "Cooking together sounds fun."

"In the meantime, would you like to go to the beach? Get some fresh air?" he asks.

"That sounds fun. Could you grab my flip-flops?"

He chuckles. "Where are they?"

"By the front door."

He retrieves my shoes and brings them back to me. I grab my keys and lock the door behind us.

"You driving?" I ask.

"We are taking a nice walk."

THE SUN BATHES THE WAVES IN A BEAUTIFUL GOLDEN LIGHT, painting the sea with its warm, gentle touch. I find myself in the company of a man who has shown me so much care and support in such a short span of time. My heart is opening up to someone new, and although it terrifies me, it's a fear I'm starting to welcome.

As Eric sits beside me on the soft sand, my gaze naturally drifts toward him. His presence beside me feels like a reassuring anchor, grounding me in the uncertainty of my own emotions. As if he can feel my eyes on him, he turns to look at me. When our eyes meet, he greets me with a tender smile. I quickly look toward the ocean, hoping he didn't catch me admiring him, but it's too late.

"You don't need to hide that beautiful face," he says.

I steal another glance at him, my heart doing a gentle dance in my chest. He's still looking at me with those kind, confident eyes of his. Eyes that seem to understand the doubts that still linger within me. But there's something in his gaze that makes me believe it's okay to be vulnerable. My fingers trace patterns in the warm sand as I gather my courage. "It's just… I've never felt this way before," I confess in a hushed tone, my voice carrying the weight of my uncertainty.

Eric reaches for my hand. "Would it comfort you to know that I share those same feelings?"

As the words linger in the air, a soft smile graces my lips, and I feel a warmth spreading through me, much like the morning sun kissing our skin. It's as though our hearts are harmonizing, beating to the same sweet melody of newfound affection.

"It does," I admit, my voice barely above a whisper. My gaze never leaves his as we share this unspoken understanding, a moment suspended in time.

Eric flashes a grin. "Well, you see, I had to consult my handbook of charming responses before saying that," he teases.

I chuckle. "Ah, the 'How to Charm Your Way into Her Heart' handbook, huh? You must have quite the collection."

He laughs, a warm, melodic sound filling the

surrounding air. "You'd be surprised," he says. "But none of them ever seemed quite right until now."

I can't help but playfully roll my eyes. "So, I'm the lucky winner of the Eric-approved response? I must be something special."

His grin widens as he leans in a little closer. "You're more than special. You're like the missing piece to a puzzle I didn't even know I had."

I feel my heart skip a beat at his words. "And here I thought I was just another piece of the beach scenery."

He leans even closer, his lips tantalizingly close to mine. "Trust me, you're the most captivating view on this beach."

My body erupts in goosebumps.

Eric stands up, his hand extended toward me. "Come on. Let's go for a swim."

I hesitate, eyeing the waves rolling in. "What? We aren't in our bathing suits!" A playful grin tugs at the corners of my lips.

He winks, his confidence unwavering. "That's the whole point, isn't it? To feel something exhilarating, something that makes our hearts race."

I can't help but laugh at his daring spirit. "You're such a daredevil," I tease, but I can feel my resolve weakening.

Eric's hand remains extended, patiently waiting. "Come on," he urges, his tone softening. "I'll keep you warm."

I accept his hand, allowing him to help me to my feet. With a grin, I follow him as we make our way toward the edge of the water. The waves on the shore, and I can feel the cool sea breeze brushing against my skin.

As the water inches closer to my feet, I pull back slightly, giggling. "Eric, I don't know about this!"

He chuckles and steps closer to me, his eyes twinkling

with amusement. "Come here," he says, his arms outstretched.

I raise an eyebrow. "What are you up to now?"

With a charming smile, he says, "I'll carry you in."

I can't help but laugh at his audacity. "You're determined to get me in this water, aren't you?"

"Absolutely. Are you ready?"

I take a deep breath, my heart racing with a mix of excitement and apprehension. "Okay, let's do it."

Eric lifts me into his arms and carries me closer to the water. I wrap my arms around his neck, feeling the warmth of his embrace in the face of the cold sea.

As Eric wades further into the ocean, the water envelopes my legs, sending shivers up my spine. I cling to him, my fingers curling around his shoulders, and I let out a laugh.

"You're a madman, Eric!"

He smirks, eyes locked onto mine as he wades deeper, the water now up to his waist. "Madly in love with making memories," he says in a voice laced with charm.

As the water touches my lower back, I let out another surprised squeal. "Okay, okay, you win! I surrender!"

Eric chuckles, and with a swift and practiced movement, he lifts me higher in his arms. "There, now you're safe," he says with a grin, his gaze never leaving mine.

"My hero." I smile.

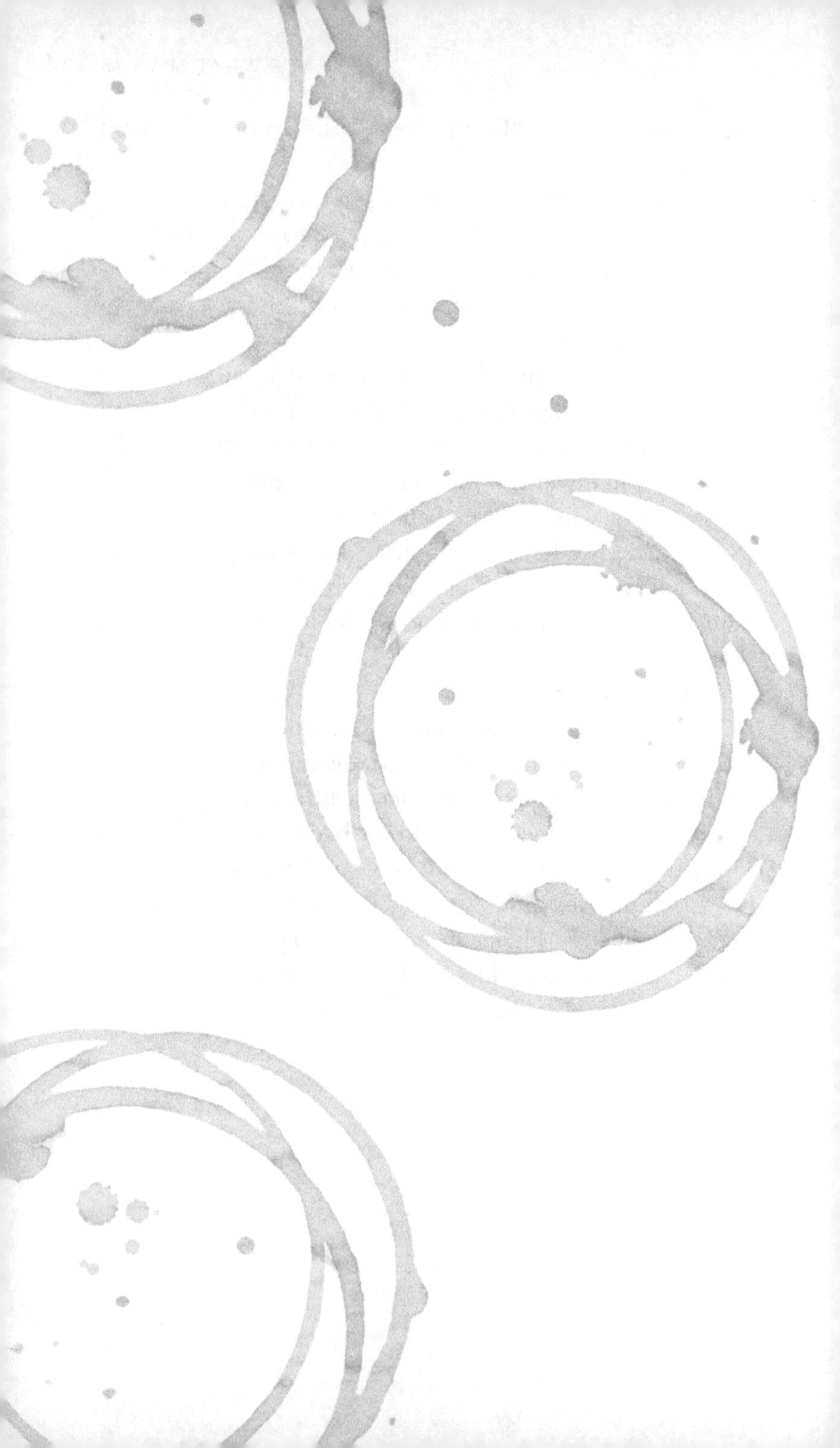

CHAPTER TWENTY-SEVEN

Still laughing and dripping wet from our ocean escapade, Eric and I walk back to my house. The sun is low, casting a warm, golden hue over everything it touches. We've been out for hours, not worried about keeping track of time. The sound of our laughter fills the air, a sweet melody that seems to echo the joy we've found in each other's company.

We reach my front door, and I turn to Eric with a mischievous grin. "Well, that was definitely an adventure."

He grins back at me, his eyes sparkling with amusement. "One for the books, for sure."

I unlock the door and push it open, revealing the cozy interior of my home. "I'm going to take a nice, warm bath to thaw out," I say, stepping inside and leaving a trail of wet footprints on the floor.

Eric follows me in, still chuckling. "That sounds like a great idea. I'll head home to shower and change before our dinner tonight."

I nod, but quickly think of a better idea. "Actually, I was thinking maybe you could shower here?"

He raises his brows. "You want me to shower here?"

I grab his hand and lead him to the bathroom, then turn on the shower. As the water warms, I take off my wet clothes, my eyes never leaving Eric's. He watches me as I undress. I step into the shower, turning away to tease him a little. He takes this as an invitation to take off his wet clothes and join me.

He steps into the warm shower, hugging me from behind, his naked body pressed against mine. My body warms, and not from the water. He whispers in my ear, "Is this what you had in mind when you suggested I shower here instead of my place?"

My legs give out on me, and if he hadn't been holding onto me, I would have ended up on the floor. I manage a small nod as I cling to Eric while I regain use of my legs. He kisses my neck just below my ear, hands roaming along my stomach and hips. His touches are feather light and send shivers up and down my spine. He whispers in my ear again, "I never want to take a shower alone again, if this is how they could be."

I turn to face him, wanting to look in his eyes when I respond. "I wouldn't mind more showers with you."

His eyes close while his hand travels down to lightly squeeze my ass. I go up on my tiptoes and gently place a kiss on his lips. He moves one of his hands to my chin and tips my face up to meet him, then deepens the kiss.

Where previous kisses were ones of passion or of tenderness, this one feels like more. It is as if words are flowing within this kiss, telling each other the extent of our true feelings. We are both starting to fall for each other, this kiss saying all the words we need to say but can't voice.

We break from the kiss and stare into each other's eyes for a long moment, standing still. "Stay the night," I say, knowing I don't want to be without him tonight.

He looks down at me and says, "I need to run home for some dry clothes and things for work in the morning, but I would absolutely love to stay the night."

"There's a key hanging by the front door. Feel free to grab it and lock the door behind you."

He gives me one last kiss as he steps out of the shower. He throws on his wet clothes, wincing as the cold begins to seep back into his bones. "I'll be back soon."

And he steps out of the bathroom, leaving me alone to think about the last few days.

ALONE, I DECIDE I WANT TO RELAX IN THE BATHTUB TO think. I turn on the water again, letting the tub fill as I step out to get a bath bomb and a glass of wine. I come back with my wine and my phone, ready to soak off the week. Stepping in, I rest the wine and my phone on the edge of the tub, and I lie back and relax, sighing deeply.

I've never felt this way about anyone. Every time his fingertips graze my skin, I experience a wave of shivers across my entire body. When I'm with him, my heart remains steady, but with every kiss, it feels like it's on a high-speed chase.

I think back over all the moments we've had, like the park and the party. Then I remember my dad coming over here and it ending in a brawl. Scrunching my nose as I recall the memory of my dad hurting him, I think of something I need to do. I reach for my phone, unlocking it. I open my contacts, tapping dad. With shaky thumbs and a sigh, I hover over the keypad and begin to type.

ME

I don't know when you'll see this message, but it's a long one, so I hope you take the time to read it. I don't know what I did for you to treat me so horribly. You have been good to me at times, but you have been awful toward me for years. I love you so much, and despite everything, I'll always be here for you. But, I can't do this anymore. The back and forth of your good and bad behavior is shattering me into pieces.

I want nothing more than to have a real father-daughter relationship with you, but I can't allow that unless you show real change. It seems the older I get, the shittier I am treated.

I take a shaky breath, pausing for a moment before continuing. Tears have already begun streaming down my face as I begin typing again.

ME

This isn't goodbye forever, but it's goodbye for now. I hope one day you find peace in your heart, because the dad who taught me how to ride a bike without training wheels, the one who taught me how to tie my shoes at such a young age, the one who bought me my first jewelry box, the one who took me to school dances and events in elementary, to field trips, I believe is still in there. I love you, Dad. Goodbye.

I finish the message and press send, deciding to block his number right after. I don't need to be hearing from him right now.

I'm so lost in the text and my emotions that I don't notice that Eric is standing in the doorway to the bathroom, waiting for me to finish. Seeing him standing there patiently makes me cry even harder. He is an example of what gentleness and kindness looks like from a man. He picks me up, wraps me in a towel, and holds me tightly to his chest on the bathroom floor.

Once my sobs have slowed, he pulls back to look at me. "Do you need anything? Water, another hug, or maybe the flowers I brought?" I look around and find a beautiful bouquet of flowers sitting next to him on the floor.

The dramatic contrast between my lifelong experiences with my dad and my current situation with Eric has left me feeling overwhelmed. Every guy in my life has turned out to be just like my dad or pale imitations of him. I learned early on not to trust guys, and Eric is obliterating those walls by sitting with me while I cry and bringing me flowers. Is this what love is?

I look back at Eric and shake my head. "No, I think I'm okay now. Thank you for being there. And for the flowers. For everything."

"Do you want me to make dinner while you relax?"

"No, I think I've done enough relaxing for now. That's what got me into this mess in the first place," I lightly joke, managing a small smile. "I'm looking forward to making dinner with you."

"So, what's for dinner, then?"

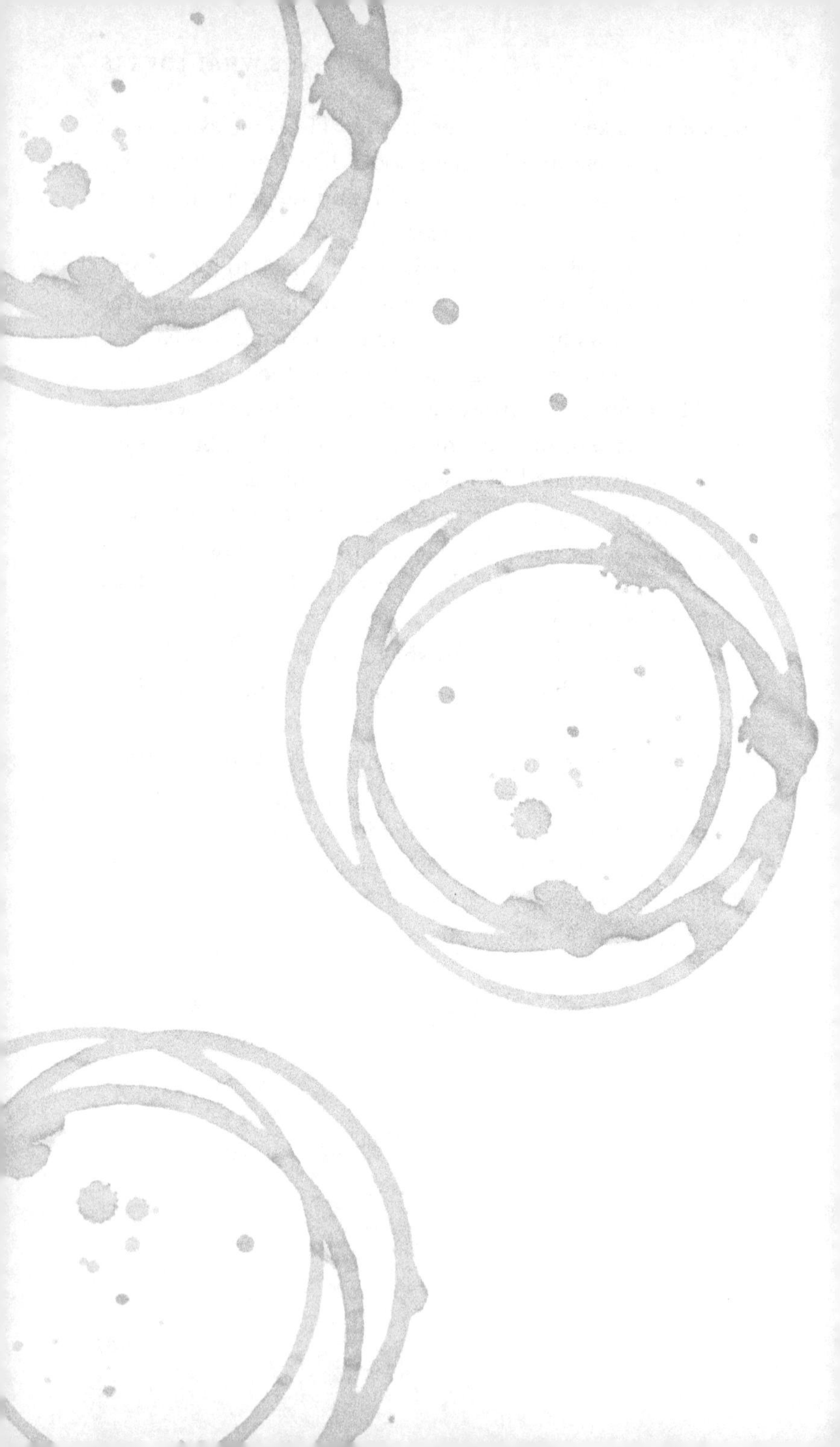

CHAPTER TWENTY-EIGHT

Standing in the kitchen, we have all the ingredients for chicken alfredo. As we begin cooking, we fall into an easy rhythm, like we have been doing together for years. With every passing minute, I feel lighter and happier. The man standing next to me has no idea the effect he has on me.

Once dinner is finished, it feels like I can almost put my dad out of my mind for now. Eric has a way of getting me out of my head and staying in the moment. We sit down for dinner, and there's a moment where I feel he might think about asking about what happened in the bathroom. I take a deep breath and pull out my phone. "When you found me in the bathroom, I had just texted my dad. This is what I sent him."

As he reads the message, his face twists in shock, his eyebrows furrowing, and his lips part slightly. His eyes darken with anger, and I can see the tension in his jaw. But as he finishes, his expression softens, and he gazes up at me with the softest smile, his eyes reflecting a deep sadness.

"I know this must be hard for you. I am proud of you

for your strength to stand up to him and do what is right for you."

He is there, he knows what was said, what my dad is like. His focus is on me and what's right for me.

He isn't trying to tear me down or tell me how I need to do things or how I am doing things wrong. He is supportive when I step out on my own, and strong for me when I need someone to lean on. I've been longing for someone to love me for me romantically, and I never believed it was possible until Eric.

"Thank you. It means a lot to me that you support me and my decision to reach out to him."

Eric looks at me with wide eyes. "All I said was I am proud of you, which I am, but that isn't anything major."

"It is to me," I whisper. "I haven't heard those words from someone in a while, and never from a guy in my life. It means a lot."

A silence descends upon the room as we both take in the moment.

Eric finally breaks the silence. "My dad meant a lot to me." He pauses. "When I lost him so suddenly at such a young age, it changed me."

I listen intently.

"I can't imagine what that must have been like for you."

Eric nods, his gaze distant as he continues, "My dad used to say those words to me all the time, you know? 'I'm proud of you.' It made me feel like I was worth something, like I was doing something right."

I reach out and place a comforting hand on his shoulder, offering silent support. It's clear that this conversation is bringing up some deep emotions for him.

He takes a deep breath and continues, "Losing him was a wake-up call. I realized that life is too short not to express how you feel about someone. So, when I said I was proud of you, I meant it. You deserve to hear those words, just like I did from my dad."

Tears well up in my eyes as I feel a mixture of sadness for his loss and gratitude for his kind words. "Thank you for sharing that with me, Eric," I manage to say, my voice filled with sincerity. "I'm grateful to have you by my side."

Eric smiles softly, his eyes reflecting the same appreciation. "Likewise," he replies tenderly. "I'm here for you, just like you're here for me, because, well, you mean the world to me."

As we sit there, the weight of our shared emotions seems to lift, replaced by a newfound bond of understanding and support. In that moment, I realize that sometimes, a simple expression of pride and the willingness to open up can create a profound connection between two people.

I place my hand on his knee, showing my support without words, and he takes it into his hand. We sit there in comfortable silence, taking in the moment. I know this is going to be a defining moment in our relationship. The big parts of our pasts are out in the open and it feels like we can take the next step forward.

In this moment, bearing our souls and supporting each other, without expectations or conditions, I start to realize, maybe this is what love is.

LETTER FROM THE AUTHOR

As I sit here, penning these final words of this passionate story, my heart is heavy with both sorrow and hope. "That's What Love Is" has been a labor of love, a journey through emotions that resonates deeply within me, and I am so grateful to have shared it with you.

This young woman, whose heart has been shattered by her father's actions, mirrors the pain I have known in my own life. While many of the events in this book were woven from the threads of imagination, I've poured some inspiration from my personal life into it.

Each word, each scene, was etched with raw emotion, for I believe that the power of storytelling lies in its ability to touch our souls and remind us of the beauty and complexity of human relationships.

If you find yourself connecting with Hailey, I hope you've found your Scarlett and Eric. And until you do, I'll be there for you.

LET'S CONNECT

Website/Newsletter:
https://www.amyroseauthor.com/

Social media:
https://www.instagram.com/amyroseauthorofficial/

Email:
hello@amyjudithrose.com

TikTok:
https://www.tiktok.com/@amyroseauthor